MARY WEEKS MILLARD

The mystery of the deserted house

DayOne

© Day One Publications 2011

First printed 2011

Reprinted 2014

ISBN 978-1-84625-272-3

All Scripture quotations, unless stated otherwise,
come from the NIV.

"NIV" is a registered trademark of
International Bible Society.
UK trademark number 1448790.

British Library Cataloguing in Publication Data available

Published by Day One Publications
Ryelands Road, Leominster, HR6 8NZ

TEL 01568 613 740   FAX 01568 611 473

email—sales@dayone.co.uk

UK web site—www.dayone.co.uk

Designed by **documen**
Printed by T J International

Dedication

For my grandson, Jason. May God bless you so much.

My grateful thanks to my publisher, Day One,
and especially to my editor, Suzanne Mitchell.

Also, my thanks to my ever patient and
loving husband, Malcolm,
for all his encouragement.

Chapter one

It was strange, really. All their lives the boys had lived in The Drive, but they had never noticed the house. It was there, of course, and they knew it was there, for they walked past it every day on their way to school or to the park. But they had never noticed it—not, that is, until the day when they lost their ball.

Joe and Matt were brothers, and they were inseparable from their best friend, Spike, who lived two doors down from them in The Drive. Spike was twelve and a half, tall, skinny and blond, with hair that always stuck up in odd places—which was why he was nicknamed 'Spike'. His real name was Nathaniel, but nobody ever called him that, except, sometimes, the teachers at school.

Matt was also twelve, but a good half a head shorter than Spike, and he hated his dark-brown hair that seemed to want to curl like a girl's! His brother, Joe, was fourteen, quiet and serious, and he hated the glasses he had to wear all the time because he was short-sighted. The three boys had formed their own gang when they were in infants' school, calling themselves 'the Whistlers' because they could all whistle well. As they grew older they made up secret messages by whistling various tunes. Spike had a little sister called Sally, and she had wanted to join the gang, but since she could not whistle, however hard she tried to learn, she was not allowed to belong. Eventually she got tired of even trying and left the boys to their own games.

It was towards the end of the Easter holidays, and the boys had set off for the park to play football. As they walked up The Drive they began to kick the ball around. They knew they were supposed to wait until they reached the park, but there were no cars in the road, so they thought it was OK. And it was OK until Matt, rather than just dribbling the ball, somehow managed to give it a mighty kick so that it sailed over the fence and into the garden of the house at the very end of The Drive. That was the moment they noticed it!

Normally they would have politely knocked on the door, apologized for kicking the ball over the fence and asked if they could retrieve it. This house, however, was deserted. It had a half-built extension over the garage, which must have been started years ago. The boys went to open the gates to the house. They were rusty and groaned as Joe opened them. For some reason, they felt a bit scared as they entered the garden, though none of them knew why.

'Come on, let's find the ball quickly,' said Spike. 'This place is a bit spooky.'

The garden was a mess. The grass hadn't been cut in years, and it took the boys a little while to locate their ball.

'Let's get out of here,' whispered Matt as he picked up the football. He didn't know why he was whispering, but the house had that sort of effect on him.

Matt and Spike quickly ran out through the gate, leaving Joe to shut it carefully before he left.

'It's funny,' Joe remarked, 'there's a Land Rover in that garden. It looks like a sculpture with those bushes growing out of it!'

'Forget it!' said Spike. 'Come on, let's get to the park!'

The Whistlers chased one another to the park and soon forgot about the house. Some other boys from their school, Veritas High, were also in the park, so they joined together and had a really good game.

It wasn't until later on that day that the boys thought about the house again. It was afternoon and they had gathered in Spike's bedroom. Matt was playing some of his favourite music. They were lounging on the bed and chatting.

'I wonder what happened to that house,' remarked Joe.

'What house?' Matt asked. His mind was on the song which he hoped would reach the top of the charts.

'That deserted house where the ball landed this morning,' replied Joe.

'Dunno,' said Spike. 'I suppose it *is* odd that it has been left like that with a half-built extension.'

'I think it's odd that it has a Land Rover left to rust in the garden,' said Joe. 'Land Rovers are so expensive and sought after.'

'When you think about it,' observed Matt, 'it's funny that it's been left there and not stolen by the gypsies who live over the road!'

The boys were quiet for a few minutes as they thought about that. There was a large gypsy settlement near The Drive. If anything went missing in the area, the crime was automatically blamed on 'the gypos', as they were nicknamed. They certainly had a scrap-metal business, and there were many old cars on their site. Joe and Matt's dad called it 'the car cemetery'! The more they thought about it, the stranger it all seemed.

'I'll tell you what,' said Spike, 'why don't we go back to the house tomorrow and do a bit of snooping around? Maybe we'll find some clues as to why it was deserted.'

'Sounds good to me,' answered Matt.

'It could be fun—we could do some detective work!' Joe added.

And so it was decided that the gang would go the next day to investigate.

Joe and Matt said goodbye to Spike, but not before Spike's mum had given them all a Coke and a home-made cookie straight from the oven. They whistled their 'see you soon' message to one another and went home.

Chapter two

It was bright and sunny the next morning, and the boys were up early.

'I take it you have something planned for today?' Matt and Joe's mum asked.

'We've arranged to meet Spike at eleven for a gang meeting,' answered Matt.

'OK, that's fine by me. You can make yourselves some sandwiches for lunch. Make some for Spike, too. Take your mobile, Joe, so that I can contact you if I need to, as I have to go shopping.'

'Thanks, Mum,' said Joe. 'A picnic sounds fun and means we can be out longer. We won't go far from home, don't worry.'

Joe felt a little guilty as he said this, for although it was quite true that they didn't plan on going far, he also knew his mum wouldn't want them to trespass in the deserted house.

He felt very responsible since he was two years older than the others. But, he reasoned, what possible harm could come to them just looking around the garden and peering through the windows? It would probably be boring anyway, and they would end up in the park playing football again!

The boys made a pile of sandwiches and Joe put them in his backpack with some drinks. Then he had a sudden thought and put in his torch, whistle and mobile. It made it seem a bit like an expedition, and you never knew when things would come in handy!

On the stroke of eleven they rang Spike's doorbell. The door was opened by his sister.

'Hi,' she said, 'have you called for Spike?'

'Yes,' the boys answered.

'We want to go out for a picnic,' Matt added.

'Can I come too?' asked Sally. Matt could have kicked himself. Of course they didn't want a little girl with them, but he hated to be so mean and tell her so.

'Not today,' said a voice from further down the hall. It was Spike's mum. 'You and I are going out, Sally. You can have a picnic another day.' Matt felt relieved when he heard that.

'Hello, Mrs Fraser,' he said. 'But is it all right if Spike joins us for a picnic? We've made it already, and we won't go far.'

'I've got my mobile with me,' said Joe, 'and I've told Mum I'll look after everyone!'

Mrs Fraser smiled as she looked at Joe's serious face. She was glad that Spike had such good friends.

'That's fine, but make sure you're home by four,' she said.

'Bring your football, Spike,' said Joe, 'in case we just end up playing at the park.'

'Good idea,' answered Spike, pulling on his hoodie and trainers.

On the way Joe said to them, 'We need to think this out and make a plan. We don't want to draw any attention to ourselves going into the house.'

'Why don't I kick the ball over the fence, like Matt did yesterday?' suggested Spike. 'Then, if any neighbours are looking around, they won't think it's suspicious.'

'Good thinking!' said Joe. 'Then I'll go through the gate and whistle "all clear", and Matt and you can join me.'

So that is what they agreed, and everything went according to plan. As they reached the end of the road and saw the house, Spike, who had been dribbling his ball, suddenly gave it a kick and landed it over the fence.

'Oh, dear! Look what you've done!' said Matt in a rather too loud voice, just in case anyone was around.

'I'll go and get it!' shouted Joe in an equally loud voice, and he headed off to open the gate.

Actually, it did seem quite scary as soon as he went into the garden. He quickly looked around, then whistled 'You'll never walk alone', and the others knew it was safe to join him. They both felt shivers go down their spines and made as little noise as they could, although they didn't know why they felt like this. It was only an old abandoned house.

The boys went round to the back garden. They figured they would be less likely to be seen there. They all felt a bit guilty at trespassing, but surely the house didn't belong to anyone. It had been deserted for years.

The Land Rover was dark green and was almost hidden by the bushes growing around it. Spike tried the driver's door, but it was locked. The tyres were flat and the bodywork rusty. They peered inside through the windows. On the back seat there was an old newspaper and some large boots.

'I wish I could see the date of that newspaper,' said
Matt. 'It would give us a clue as to when it was last used!'

'We could break the window,' suggested Spike.

'No!' said Joe firmly. 'Let's not cause any damage.
We've got a lot to explore. Maybe we can find other clues
somewhere else.'

Grass and weeds were growing everywhere, but among
them were some lovely plants. Joe loved gardens and
plants, so he noticed them. He stopped and looked at a
large tree covered in tiny yellow balls of blossom.

'Whew!' he exclaimed to the others. 'Look at that! A
beautiful mimosa tree, the yellow Australian Wattle!' Spike
and Matt looked at it but were unimpressed. All trees
looked the same to them, apart from chestnuts when the
conkers ripened!

'Forget the plants!' said Matt to his brother. 'Let's see
the house!'

They were walking through long grass near the back
door when Matt almost screamed. He had disturbed a
snake, and his heart began to beat very loudly in his
chest. The boys froze as they watched the snake quickly
slither away.

'From its markings, I'm sure that was an adder!' said
Spike. 'Thank goodness it didn't bite us!'

'Well, it's gone now,' said Joe, trying not to show how
frightened he had felt. 'Let's go on.'

They walked on to the back door. Matt tried the door,
but it was locked. He peered through the window and was
disappointed that there was nothing much to see. There
was just a hallway, a few coats on some pegs and another
pair of boots.

Joe was looking at the half-built extension above the garage. 'Why would anyone leave it half-finished?' he wondered. 'It doesn't make sense.' He shivered. He couldn't get away from the feeling that it was all a bit spooky. He wanted to tell the others to forget exploring, but somehow he couldn't. The house must hold some secrets somewhere!

Spike had made his way a little further round the back and called out to them. 'Look,' he said, 'I can open this window. The hinges have become so rusty that it will push open and we can climb in!'

'Should we do this?' asked Matt. He had really had quite a scare over the adder and wasn't feeling quite so brave any more.

'I'm not sure,' said Joe. 'But I guess it won't hurt. It's not like it belongs to anyone now.'

He took off his backpack and gave it to Spike to hold while he carefully clambered through the window into a very small, dark room.

Chapter three

'Are you OK?' Spike asked Joe.

'Yes, but it's a bit dark in here. I think I'm in a cupboard.' Joe flashed his torch around and saw that there were shelves with some tins on them. He tried the door. The handle creaked as Joe opened it. He whistled to the others to join him and they carefully climbed through the small window too.

Joe had found the kitchen. The boys blew the dust off the chairs and table and sat down.

'It feels weird,' said Matt in a quiet voice.

'Why are you whispering?' asked Spike.

'I don't know,' replied Matt. 'I've got a feeling that someone might come out of another room at any moment and find us.'

'That's silly,' said Joe, 'but I know what you mean. It's as if this house still belongs to somebody.'

'Well,' said Spike, 'I feel hungry. Can we have our picnic now?'

The boys looked at one another. 'Well, I suppose it wouldn't hurt,' said Joe, and began to get the food out of the backpack. Once they began to eat the boys felt better and started to talk in normal voices.

'Shall we explore the whole house?' Matt asked.

'I've got a notebook—I thought we could write down any clues we find that might help us to solve the mystery,' said Joe. 'My first note is about the Land Rover. The sort of person who would drive a Land Rover might be a farmer.'

'Or maybe just someone from the country,' Matt said.

Joe wrote the suggestions down in his book. 'Anyone thought of anything else?' he asked.

'Well,' said Matt, 'you said something about that tree in the garden.'

'You're right,' Joe answered. 'These people must be good gardeners or have travelled and collected exotic plants.'

'Maybe they're Australians,' suggested Spike, remembering what Joe had called the tree.

'Hey, this is great! Look at all these notes we've been able to make already!' Joe was getting excited. 'Come on, let's look around this room and see what else we can deduce.'

So the three boys began to look in the kitchen cupboards. When Matt opened one there was a scurrying noise that made them all jump, but then they laughed at themselves when they saw the culprit was just a tiny mouse.

'There are cupboards with tins and packets of food,' said Matt, adding, 'though lots of the packets have been eaten by mice, and when you touch them, the cardboard dissolves into dust!'

'That means that the people left the house expecting to return and use the food,' deduced Spike.

'It certainly looks like that,' said Joe. 'But it must have

been ages ago, judging by the state of these packets.'

'The fridge is empty and switched off,' said Spike, 'and my mum does that when we go away for some time.'

'They didn't turn off the water, though,' remarked Joe. 'When I turned on the tap, a trickle of brown water came out!'

'The lights don't work,' said Matt, after trying a switch.

The boys thought about this for a moment and then Spike said, 'I know: if you don't pay the bills, then the gas and electricity get switched off. Maybe the water is switched off at the mains too, and there's just a trickle left in the pipes.'

Joe duly wrote all these clues down in his notebook.

'We've learnt loads from just this room,' he said. 'I know, let's all come up with a story as to what could have happened to the people! We could come again tomorrow and bring our suggestions. In fact, why don't we make this our gang den? It could be the home of the Whistlers!'

'That'll be all right through the summer, but I bet it's cold in the winter!' said Matt.

'We've got all the summer term and the holidays before we have to worry about that,' answered Joe. 'But it'd be a great place for us now!'

The boys nodded in agreement. Up until then the gang had had to meet in their bedrooms. It would be great to have a place of their own, a secret place!

'I can't come tomorrow, though,' said Spike. 'It's Sunday, and you know I go to church and my grandparents come round for dinner.'

'But we start back at school on Monday,' said Matt. 'Do you have to go to church? Isn't it a bit sissy, anyway?

Surely your parents don't make you go!'

Spike hesitated. He really wanted to be with the gang and explore the rest of the house. He also hated being thought 'sissy' for going to church, but it was hard to explain, even to his best friends, that he actually didn't mind going. In fact, he even looked forward to Sundays. He was so tempted to say 'yes' and promise to come to the house the next day, but he knew deep down that he had to stand up for what he knew was right.

'Mum and Dad don't make me go to church. I actually like going, and we have a great youth group. I really want to explore this house, but just not tomorrow.' Spike realized he was going a little pink with embarrassment as he said this, and he was glad that the kitchen was rather dark so his friends wouldn't see.

Matt was about to try to persuade Spike to forget church when Joe butted in. 'That's OK, Spike,' he said. 'The evenings are getting lighter, and we can have our gang meetings here then. Actually, perhaps we shouldn't come every day anyway, or we may be noticed, and then our secret place won't be ours any more. We'll have to be very careful that we come and go quietly.'

Spike was relieved that Matt and Joe accepted his decision to go to church, and in his heart he whispered a 'thank you' to God. The last few months he had begun to really enjoy his youth group and had started to read his Bible and try to understand more about Christianity.

Joe started to sneeze and he felt his chest tighten.

'Let's get out of here,' he said. 'I need my inhaler. The dust is affecting me.' He reached into his backpack and took two good puffs of his inhaler. The boys went back to the cupboard and out through the tiny window. Joe went first and made sure the coast was clear before he whistled for the others to follow. They collected their ball from the garden and slipped out through the gate, glad that nobody was walking up The Drive at that moment.

'Let's go and have a quick game of football,' suggested Matt. 'Then we can tell our mums that we were playing in the park, and it will help keep our gang hideaway secret.'

'Good idea!' said Joe and Spike together. The boys raced around the corner and into the park.

Chapter four

The first week of the summer term was so busy that the boys couldn't have a gang meeting until the next Saturday.

Joe and Matt called for Spike as soon as they could after lunch, and they did their usual trick with the ball. A few people were walking past, but nobody took any notice of the boys as they opened the gate of the deserted house and whistled to one another. They went carefully round to the back of the house. Spike reached the window first and deftly let himself in, followed quickly by the others. Since they were going to make it their den, they had each brought things to kit it out. They put torches, string and essential rations like Coke and crisps on the shelf in the cupboard, making sure that everything was in tins and mice-proof.

They made their way into the kitchen and sat down. They were all feeling a bit bolder now that they had made the house their den.

'What shall we do first?' asked Matt.

'I think we should look in another room and then share our stories,' answered Spike.

'OK,' responded Joe, 'but I like to think we're detectives, so we're going to share our theories rather than made-up stories!'

'Let's go into the other downstairs rooms,' Joe said, and the others nodded. He led the way, and they followed him down a passageway from which three doors and a staircase led off.

The first door was very stiff and made a grating noise as it opened. The boys were disappointed to find it was just a toilet! Joe had his pencil and notebook at the ready.

'One toilet and hand basin,' he wrote. 'White toilet paper, chewed by mice!'

The boys closed the door and went to the door on the left side of the passage. It opened more easily, but once again they heard a scuttling sound.

'It's only mice—we must expect that,' said Joe, hoping it really was only mice and not rats. The boys gazed at the room, taking it all in. It was a dining-room. In the middle was a dark-brown table, with six chairs around it. Layers of dust covered them. Against one wall was a sideboard, and against another, a large bookcase and a desk. In the window was a small table with a lamp.

'There must be lots of clues here!' exclaimed Spike. 'My dad always says you can tell a lot about a person if you look at their books!' He made his way to the bookcase. As he touched a book, dust went spiralling all over the room, causing Joe to start coughing.

'Sorry, Joe,' he said, 'I forgot about your asthma.'

'Let's go back to the kitchen, let the dust settle, then come back and look at the books,' suggested Matt.

Joe was coughing badly and needed his inhaler, so the

boys quickly went back to the kitchen and sat down there.

When Joe had stopped coughing, Spike announced, 'Now I'm going to tell you my theory about this house! I think a family lived here,' he began.

'How d'you know that?' interrupted Matt. 'We haven't been upstairs and seen the bedrooms yet!'

'I didn't need to go upstairs to work that out,' Spike replied. 'You see, here in the kitchen there are lots of plates and knives and forks and things, including some children's plates, and over there in the corner there's a high chair.'

'Good deduction!' said Joe approvingly.

'Well,' continued Spike, 'this family must have been growing too big for the house, so the parents decided that they needed to have an extension built. It costs an awful lot to have one built—my dad was talking about it the other day. So the father was worried about money. Then he had an idea. He would play the Lottery and see if he could win. It would solve all his problems. So he played and, amazingly, he won, becoming a millionaire overnight!

'After that, letters started to arrive and all kinds of charities asked for money. Even relatives he'd never heard of began to call and ask for help.

'He talked to his wife. How could they solve their new problem? The extension was going up fast. He'd been able to buy the Land Rover he'd always wanted. He'd even bought beautiful plants for the garden. But he wasn't happy, because everyone kept pestering him for money. He decided that life had been better when he was poor. Even his growing family were always asking for new clothes and toys, and weren't content any more. His wife felt the same way.

'"This money's a curse!" she said. "What on earth can we do to escape?"

'"That's it! You've just given the answer: we'll escape!" the man replied.

'"How?" asked his wife.

'"We'll pack up as if we're going on holiday, and we'll just disappear. We can travel until we find a place we like, a place where nobody knows us and we can live quietly. Then, when everyone has forgotten all about us and our money, we can return and live here again!"'

'So,' continued Spike, 'that's what they did. They told their children to pack up to go on holiday, but they didn't tell anyone where they were going or that they might not come back for years. So this house is waiting for them to return.'

'Wow!' said Joe, 'That's a brilliant theory! We must write it down in the notebook.'

Just then, Joe's mobile rang. They all nearly jumped out of their skins!

'Hi, Mum,' he answered. 'Sorry ... I forgot the time ... we'll be home in five minutes ... we're just at the end of The Drive!'

They had all been so engrossed in Spike's theory that they had forgotten the time! Quickly they put their things back on the cupboard shelf and let themselves out through the window, one by one. As before, Joe went round to the front to make sure the coast was clear, then whistled to the others to follow. They picked up their ball and ran down The Drive.

Chapter five

It was the end of lunch-break at school the following Tuesday and Spike had been to the Christian Union meeting for the first time. In his heart Spike knew that he really wanted to be a Christian. He had never thought much about God until recent months. He had never doubted that there was a God, and he knew that his parents talked to God a lot, but God had never seemed real to Spike. During the past few months, however, Spike had become increasingly aware that he needed to choose whether he was going to become a real Christian with God as a part of his life, or forget it all and stop going to church. When Matt had challenged him that time about whether he was going to go to church or to the gang meeting, Spike knew that he wanted to go to church. He wanted to really know God. That had led to his joining the CU at school.

Spike had enjoyed the meeting. It was led by a girl from year eleven, and there seemed to be more girls than boys in the group, but one boy was there whom Spike knew from church. At the meeting, a prison officer had talked about prisoners finding faith in the nearby men's prison. It really impressed Spike that former hardened criminals now loved God.

Spike was very thoughtful as he made his way across the yard to the science block for his afternoon class. He didn't take much notice as a group of about five boys came alongside him. They cornered him and pinned him against the wall.

'Who's a namby-pamby sissy then!' they jeered. 'Who's mummy's good boy who goes to church?'

One boy hit him on the side of his face. 'Turn the other cheek, sissy boy, and let me hit the other side. Isn't that what the Bible tells you to do?'

Spike was scared. These boys were from his year group and were known to be bullies. Even though the school had strict policies about bullying, this gang managed to intimidate kids from time to time both inside and outside school.

'God, please help me!' he shouted in his head, then he let out an almost involuntary whistle like a scared blackbird. It was the distress signal that the Whistlers had practised over and over for fun but had never had to use.

Spike couldn't see over the heads of these big boys who were pinning him to the wall, but while they continued to jeer at him, Joe came up. Having heard the distress signal, he realized that either Matt or Spike was in trouble, and he angrily spoke to the bullies.

'What d'you think you're doing? I'm going to report you at once!'

The group looked round at Joe and backed off. He might be quite small and wear glasses, but he was a prefect and two years their senior. They knew he had authority and could get them into serious trouble.

'So what if this boy attends church?' Joe shouted at them. 'I don't think you'd attack Ali Khan for attending the mosque!' Ali was a large boy who was well known in the school for his boxing ability!

'What difference does it make if he goes to church?' Joe continued. 'We should all be allowed our beliefs, and going to church doesn't make you a sissy!' By now Joe was really angry, and the bullies were such cowards that they began to walk away from Spike.

'Anyone would think you were one of the God Squad too!' muttered one of the bullies as he walked away.

'I don't do church, but I'm thinking of trying. I'd certainly rather be a person like Spike than end up like one of you!' was Joe's parting comment to the boy.

Spike picked up his bag. His shirt had been torn by the bullies, and he tried to tidy himself up, ready for his next class.

'Are you OK, Spike?' asked Joe. He could see that the younger boy was shaking.

'Yes, I'm OK now,' answered Spike. 'Thank you for speaking up for me. I really appreciate that, Joe. They must have seen me come from the CU meeting. I went there for the first time this lunch-break, and it had really made me think. I didn't even notice that gang coming over the yard. I guess I'll be in more trouble at home when Mum sees this shirt!' he added ruefully.

The bell rang and the two boys ran off in different directions to their classes. As they parted Joe called out, 'I'll see you at the gates after school in case those bullies are waiting for you!'

Spike found it hard to concentrate during the science lesson. He was glad that the bullies, although in the same year group, were not in his science group. He realized that if he made a Christian commitment, he would be a target for ridicule by some of the other pupils at school. Was it worth it? Yet he was also aware that he had called out to God to help him in a difficult situation and, without any doubt, God had heard and helped! How cool was that! God coming to his rescue in the shape of Joe! What would Joe think if he knew God had used him? Did Joe mean it when he said he might go to church? All these thoughts were going round and round in his head. Eventually the bell went and the lesson finished.

'Nathaniel Fraser, please wait behind after the lesson,' he heard his science teacher call out.

'Now what?' Spike thought to himself. 'As if there's not been enough trouble today!'

'Sir?' he said to his teacher.

'What's happened to your shirt?' the teacher asked. 'It's not like you to be so untidy.'

Spike didn't want to grass on the boys who had bullied him.

'Well, sir,' he answered, 'it got torn when I fell against the wall in the yard.'

'Really?' asked the teacher. 'If there's been any foul play out there, I want you to tell me.'

Spike could tell that his teacher was not really satisfied with his answer, but he decided to say no more.

'Yes, sir, I will,' he answered.

'Off you go then,' said the teacher, and Spike was only too glad to get on his way home.

True to his word, Joe was waiting for him, along with Matt. When they saw Spike emerge from the locker room they whistled the 'all clear' and he knew that the bullies were not waiting for him. Spike felt relieved. How good it was to have friends like Joe and Matt!

As they walked down The Drive together, Joe told Matt about the trouble that Spike had run into in the lunch hour. He then turned to Spike and said, 'I did mean it, Spike, when I said I might try coming to church one Sunday. I admire you, standing up for what you believe in.'

'You can go, but don't expect me to come,' declared Matt. 'You're great guys, but I don't want to go to any boring old church!'

'That's OK,' said Spike, 'you're the best mates anyone could have and I'm proud to belong to the Whistlers!'

Spike was glad to get home and change out of his school clothes. It had been a strange day, both good and bad. Mum was in the kitchen and he decided he had better tell her about the torn shirt.

Mrs Fraser knew instantly, in the way that mums do, that Spike had something on his mind. She got him a Coke from the fridge.

'I'm about to have a cup of tea,' she said. 'Why don't we sit down together and you can tell me about your day. I've got a bit of time before I have to collect Sally from her dance rehearsal. By the way, it's really great of you to say you'll come and see her dance on Saturday.'

'That's OK,' said Spike. 'Actually, Mum, I want to talk to you about a lot of things. First, I am so sorry, but my school shirt is torn!'

'Maybe you'd better tell me all about it before I get

cross!' said his mum, smiling.

Spike began to tell her about going to the CU at school, then the trouble in the yard, his prayer and Joe's help. He found that his mum was really listening, so he went on to tell her how he had been thinking about wanting to know God for himself.

After Spike had finished talking, he looked up at his mum to see if she was cross about the shirt. She was quiet for a few minutes, but still smiling lovingly at him.

'Spike,' she said, 'I don't mind how many shirts get torn if it means you come to know God in a real way. I have prayed since before you were born that you would become a Christian and follow Jesus. There is no greater thing I want for any of my children. Of course I want you to be happy and do well at school, but the greatest thing in all our lives is to know and love God.

'Now, about this bullying, I understand you don't want any trouble or revenge. However, it is a serious thing and if it does happen again, will you promise to tell me, so that we can at least decide together what to do about it?'

'Yes, Mum, I promise, and thanks for being so understanding. I haven't made up my mind exactly about being a Christian, but I really am thinking about it.' Spike smiled at his mum.

That evening in his bedroom, Spike tried to think through all the events of the day. He decided to write things down in a notebook, just as Joe did. He underlined two things:

1. *Prisoners wanted to follow Jesus.*
2. *God heard my cry for help.*

He deduced that God must really care about him. He
was aware that he had a choice to make. Mum had said
that the best thing she could want for her children was that
they would choose to follow Jesus. Spike knew that being
in a Christian family did not make anyone a Christian, not
even somebody who had been baptized. You had to make
a choice. Spike also knew that he had often done wrong
things which the Bible called 'sin'. He knew that, just as
he was, he could never go to heaven. He remembered how,
one morning not long before, he had woken a bit late and
found that nobody was in the house. He was terrified! Mum
and Dad were not in their room, neither was Sally in hers.
He had gone downstairs and looked in all the rooms, but no
one was there. He had thought that the end of the world
had come and Jesus had taken the family to heaven, but he
had been left behind because he was not a Christian! Then
he opened the back door to find all the family chasing a
chicken that had escaped from its run! Spike remembered
his huge relief that it wasn't too late for him and the end of
the world hadn't arrived yet! It was that that had started
him thinking seriously about following Jesus.

Having written lots of things in his notebook, Spike
decided to talk to God about it.

'Dear Lord, first of all I want to say thank you because
you answered my prayer in school today. Then I want to
say how cool it is that hardened criminals in the prison love
you—they certainly aren't sissies! I really want to know
you and I am choosing to follow you. I know I am not much
good and have messed up so often. I feel bad about myself,
but I'm truly sorry and ask you to forgive me, Jesus. If
you can use a guy like me, please make me a Christian. By

the way, I'm not very brave, so please can you keep those bullies away? And I'm sorry to ask so much, but belonging to the Whistlers also means a lot to me, so please can Joe and Matt also become Christians? Amen.'

Spike felt a strange feeling of warmth and happiness, and deep down he had a strong sense that Jesus had answered his prayer. He wrote down in his notebook, 'I prayed, and God has made me a Christian, and it feels cool!'

When he had written that, he laughed to himself and thought, 'Well, actually, it feels warm, not cool!'

Chapter six

The next Saturday came at last and the gang met at the house. Joe had gone on ahead because he was very curious to look at some of the books on the shelves in the dining-room. He had taken an extra dose of his inhaler and he handled the books with great care. He deduced that whoever owned the house was interested in travelling, because there were books about other countries. There were also some history books, and many English classics. The bottom shelf held a variety of young children's books and several videos. He noted that there seemed to be no DVDs. Maybe the people had left the house before the invention of DVDs? Joe duly noted all his deductions and thoughts in his notebook, ready to share his findings with Matt and Spike when they arrived.

Before long, he heard their whistles to announce their arrival, and he whistled the 'all clear' signal back. Spike went in first, and Matt followed him after a few minutes. As Matt waited to hear his whistle signal, he thought he saw a net curtain move just a little in the house next door. It made him feel nervous, and he looked very carefully, but he saw nothing. He decided it was probably just his imagination.

In the kitchen Joe updated the others on the books he had investigated. They talked about them together. The selection seemed to confirm the theory that there had been children living in the house.

It also suggested that the people who had lived there were interested in other countries. When they discussed the English classics and poetry books, Spike suggested that perhaps one of the parents was an English teacher.

Matt was keen to explore upstairs, so Spike and Joe agreed. The stairs creaked as they walked up, and on the top landing there was a hole cut out of the wall and covered with a now very tatty piece of tarpaulin. This was obviously where the extension joined.

'Fancy going away and leaving the top floor open!' was Matt's comment.

'I wonder if they had to leave in a hurry?' pondered Joe. 'Otherwise, surely they would've had the builders put in a door before they left!'

'That's another clue to put in the notebook,' said Spike.

The first door off the landing was a bathroom. There was nothing very unusual to be found there. The landing had three other doors. The boys opened the first door and whistled in surprise! It was a young boy's room, with blue wallpaper with trains on it. The curtains and bedspread matched, and all the toys were arranged neatly. On a small table was a photo of a little boy with a wide smile and curly hair. The boys thought he looked about three years old. Beside the photo was a half-used candle.

'This room feels very sad to me!' observed Joe. 'The little boy looks happy in the photo, but there is something odd and sad about it all.'

'It's made me feel cold!' said Matt. 'Perhaps it's haunted!'

'It's just too tidy!' remarked Spike. 'Even when we go away, our bedrooms don't look as tidy as this. It doesn't look as if it was ever lived in!'

'Let's go back to the kitchen, have a snack and write up what we've seen and how we feel while it's still fresh in our minds,' said Joe. 'Afterwards, Matt can give us his theory as to what happened for this house to become deserted.'

The other two readily agreed. They went back down to the kitchen and munched away while Joe wrote up their notes and comments in the book. When he closed it, Spike turned to Matt and asked him to start his story as he had to get home early.

Matt began, 'My theory is this. A young couple were travelling the world. They came from Australia and, although they loved their home, they wanted to see the world.'

'That would make sense,' said Spike, 'because of the Wattle tree!'

'Exactly!' said Matt. 'I was just coming to that. They loved their home so much that they had a little Wattle tree planted in a tin, which they took everywhere they went. It was a sort of good-luck charm. However, in England they ran out of money, so they couldn't get back home. They decided to work and save to go back to Australia. They soon got good jobs and began to save. Then the woman found out that she was pregnant. At first it was OK and she continued to work, but then she fell sick and had to stop work. They were living in one room and knew that they would have to find somewhere better before the baby was born. The man worked very hard and his boss told him that if he would stay in the firm for five years, then he could have a rise and start to buy a house. It seemed to be the answer to their problem, so the young couple began to buy this house.

'They had their baby and others followed, until even this house was getting too small and they needed more rooms. The family then decided to stay in England because the children were used to England and had friends here. However, the couple missed Australia so much that they planted their Wattle tree in the garden so that it would always remind them of their homeland. They also bought a Land Rover because it reminded them of driving over vast distances in the bush.

'They now had too many children and too many expenses in their house for them to think of returning to Australia. Then, one day, something happened. A telegram arrived. They used to have telegrams years ago,' Matt added in explanation.

'This telegram said that the man's father was seriously ill and longed to see him and his family before he died. He asked them all to return, and said that he would pay all expenses. The family packed their cases and told the builders to stop work until they returned. They locked up the house and flew to Australia. When they got there, they found the man's father had already died, but no money was left to pay for their expenses.

'Now the family were in Australia with no money to return to England. The man also now had to care for his mother. They wanted to return to England. They always intended to return one day and finish building the house, so they didn't sell it. But the children grew to love Australia, and somehow it was never the right time to return as one or another child was always taking exams at school—so they just never came back! So the house was deserted!'

Matt took a deep breath at the end of his story. 'That's what I think could have happened!' he declared.

'Well done!' said Spike. 'I think that's a really good theory!'

'I do, too,' Joe said. 'It makes sense of the Wattle tree, the Land Rover and the travel books.'

'I really need to go home now,' said Spike. 'Shall we meet next Saturday?'

'Yes,' answered Joe, 'but maybe I'll come to church with you tomorrow morning.'

'Knock on our door about 9.30,' said Spike. 'It'll be really cool if you can come!'

Spike let himself out through the cupboard window, looked around to check that the coast was clear, and ran down The Drive. He could hardly believe what Joe had said!

Matt was the next to leave the house, and he looked anxiously to see if the net curtains moved next door, but he saw nothing. He was very pleased with himself because he had worried all week about making a theory about the deserted house. The others had liked his ideas and he felt good!

Joe tidied up the kitchen, taking away the empty cans and crisp bags. They would have to be careful not to be noticed, he thought to himself. Joe was always very observant, and his father used to tease him and say he would end up being a detective!

Chapter seven

When Joe got home he went straight up to his room. He could not forget the boy's room they had discovered in the deserted house. It had felt like a very private place which they shouldn't have seen. It had also felt a very sad place.

Joe knew that the next time the gang met he would have to share his theory about the house. Each time they visited it, his ideas changed. He was bothered that the gypsies had not stolen the Land Rover, even though they were notorious for stealing cars in the area.

All these thoughts were going round in his head. He was also thinking about his promise to Spike. Why had he said he would go to church with him? The event in the school-yard earlier in the week had really angered him. Bullying always made Joe very angry. It was partly because of that incident that Joe had said he would go with Spike. He thought that it might sort of make things a bit better for him. Joe thought it was strange that Spike somehow seemed happier since the bullies attacked him than he had before! He was intrigued. There must be something in Christianity that was worth standing up for. He thought he would like to learn a bit more about it.

Sunday morning was wet. Joe reluctantly got up and dressed. He had told his parents that he was going to church with Spike. They were mildly surprised but had no objections. They knew that the Frasers were church-goers and they respected them for it.

Joe knocked on the Frasers' door and Spike was delighted to see him. 'I thought you might not come as it's so wet,' he commented.

'I promised I would,' Joe replied, 'and a promise is a promise!'

Joe was very surprised by his experience of the church. It was not at all as he had expected. There was a really good band playing modern songs as well as hymns. Joe didn't know any of the songs, but the words were on a screen and he found it easy to follow them. Some of the tunes were very catchy. The service certainly wasn't boring. After about half an hour, the young people went out to their own groups. Joe found it all very interesting, and quickly forgetting his shyness, he asked the leader questions. Apart from during RE classes at school, he had never really thought about God at all. For him, it was a completely new idea that a person could know God as a friend. All in all, Joe was very impressed. He thought he might try to go with Spike most Sundays.

At lunch-time, Matt asked Joe if church had been boring, and Joe told him that it had actually been interesting and fun. When he told Matt about the band, Matt's eyes lit up because he was longing to learn the drums.

'D'you think you'll go again?' Matt inquired.

'Possibly,' answered Joe, not too keen to let everyone know that he was really interested; but actually he had already made up his mind to try to go regularly.

Since Spike had asked Jesus to come into his life, he had felt really different. It wasn't a feeling he could easily put into words, but he had a sense deep down inside that he was at peace and safe. He had started to talk to Jesus, telling him all about school, the gang and pretty much everything that was going on. Every morning he asked for help for the day, especially that he would have the courage to stand up for his faith if the bullies mocked him again. Thankfully, they hadn't bothered him since that first time.

Now Spike knew that he wanted to ask God for something else. He wanted to say 'thank you' that Joe had come to church with him, but he wanted to ask that he would keep coming, and that Matt would want to join them too. He wanted them to become real Christians. Wouldn't it be great, he thought, if all the gang were Christians!

Chapter eight

During the next week, each time he passed the deserted house Matt glanced at the house next door. He had an uncanny feeling that he was being watched, although he could not see anybody and he did not see the net curtain move again. Saturday arrived and the gang met as usual.

The boys went in one by one, whistling to one another to signal that all was well. Once in the kitchen Matt voiced his fears that they were being watched by someone in the next-door house.

'Perhaps one of us should come down The Drive before we meet and hang around a bit by that house or on the other side of the road,' suggested Joe.

'Well, I could do that next time,' offered Spike. 'I could even bring Spot with me and pretend he was having a walk.' Spot was the Frasers' Jack Russell terrier. 'I could quickly take him home after you'd both arrived.'

'If you don't mind doing that, I think it would be less suspicious than you hanging around here on your own,' said Joe.

'All right then, that's settled,' said Spike.

'Let's go upstairs and look at the other bedrooms,' said Matt; he wanted to get on with the exploring.

'OK,' replied Joe and Spike together, and the boys went up the creaky staircase. Even though they had visited the deserted house several times now, it still felt a bit spooky. They passed the boy's bedroom and went into the room opposite. It was large and looked out onto the front garden. Somehow, in spite of the dust, it felt more comfortable and 'lived in' than the boy's room. There was a large double bed with bedside tables. One wall had fitted cupboards and against another wall there was a dressing table.

Matt went to open the cupboards. Spike was a bit uncomfortable with this at first.

'It seems rude to open someone's private cupboards,' he commented. Joe hesitated too, but then he decided that as they had explored other bookshelves and cupboards, they might as well look inside these cupboards, otherwise they might miss some vital clues. Reluctantly, Spike agreed.

There were some clothes, mostly women's garments, hanging from a rail. Other items were in a heap, and some were tidily put into drawers.

'Whoever lived here meant to come back,' noted Joe, 'otherwise they would have taken all their clothes. Nearly all the clothes seem to be women's, but there is a suit hanging up and a few ties.'

'There really aren't many clues in this room,' said Matt in a rather disappointed voice. 'Let's go on to the last bedroom.'

The boys shut the cupboard doors and left the room exactly as they had found it and then went into the third bedroom. This one was much smaller. It was not very interesting at all; just a bed, chest of drawers, a small wardrobe and a chair.

'I guess this is a guest-room,' commented Spike. 'It doesn't look "lived in" at all.'

He walked over to the chest of drawers and was going to open the top drawer when he drew in his breath sharply.

'Look!' he said in an excited voice. 'Although there's dust everywhere, just as in all the other rooms, someone has been in here! There are fingerprints in the dust, and even though they're also dusty, you can still see them!'

Matt and Joe went over to see.

'Don't touch anything!' warned Joe. 'They may be important clues.'

'Clues to what?' Matt asked. He just wanted to explore.

'I don't know,' said Joe, 'but I think we ought to shut the door at least for now and go downstairs to think about it!'

'I agree,' said Spike. 'Anyway, it's time for a snack!'

The boys returned to the kitchen. Matt went to the store cupboard to get their rations.

Once they had finished eating and drinking, Joe got out his notebook.

'We haven't really got many new clues,' he commented, 'but we'll write down what we have deduced.'

Matt started: 'We went into the parents' bedroom and it seemed they had left, meaning to return.'

'And for some reason, there were very few men's clothes, and lots of women's,' added Spike.

'Our dad would say that was normal!' joked Joe.

'Joe, it's your turn to come up with a theory now,' chipped in Matt.

'OK,' replied Joe. 'But let's finish this first. We need to write about the other room.'

'Not much to say about that,' replied Matt. 'It appears to be the guest-room. We didn't look inside the wardrobe or chest of drawers, but Spike found fingerprints that were newer than the dust.'

'They were still from some time ago,' commented Spike. 'Someone has been into that room and touched that chest of drawers since the house became deserted.'

'Maybe it was the builder, wanting to be paid,' Matt suggested.

'We haven't thought about the builder, have we?' said Joe thoughtfully. 'That's a whole new avenue to explore. If we knew who the builder was, then maybe we could learn more.'

'That'll have to wait until another gang meeting,' said Spike. 'I want to hear your theory before we go home. Time is getting on!'

'All right,' began Joe. 'I was puzzled because the gypsies hadn't taken the Land Rover. I felt there had to be some reason why they haven't taken things from here. The more I thought about what we've seen, the more I felt that the boy's room was somehow spooky, like a shrine. I think that the little boy either got sick, or was in some sort of accident, and died.'

'It certainly did feel spooky,' agreed Spike. 'And the other bedrooms don't feel like that.'

'I thought about that a lot,' continued Joe. 'It must be terrible when a child dies, but it does happen sometimes. I wonder if the mother couldn't cope with the death of her child, and so made his room like a shrine. I think that maybe she was still so unhappy that one day she committed suicide.'

'Why do you think that?' asked Matt.

'Because the gypsies wouldn't go near a house where a suicide had been committed. It would be like a curse on the house. There has to be some reason why they haven't taken the Land Rover. They live so near that they would know the history. That also might explain why the women's clothes are all left here. Perhaps with all the tragedy, the husband, having lost both his son and his wife, decided to quit the house and maybe travel the world—or, if he was from Australia as Spike thought, just went back there. Maybe he could never face returning here because of the memories.'

'What a sad theory!' exclaimed Spike. 'But there is definitely a great feeling of spookiness and sadness in this house, especially upstairs.'

'D'you think she hanged herself here?' whispered Matt. He looked around, almost as if he expected to see a ghost walk in.

'I've no idea, it's just my theory,' replied Joe.

'And on that sad note, I think we should call the Whistlers' gang meeting over!' declared Spike. He wanted everyone to cheer up and go home.

They left the house one by one. It was easier now because Joe had brought some oil and the gate didn't squeak any more. Somehow, today, they were all glad to get out into the sunshine again. It had been a weird morning.

Chapter nine

The following week Spike began to take Spot for a
walk along The Drive every day. He tried to go before
school, quite early in the morning. It was very quiet,
with no one about except the milkman doing his round,
and he didn't notice anything unusual—that is, until the
Friday. As he waited at the end of The Drive that day, he
noticed the front door being opened in the house next to
the deserted house, the one where Matt had thought he
had seen the net curtain move. A very old man, almost
bent double, came out of the house and picked up his milk.
He briefly looked around and stared at Spike, then went
indoors again.

'At least we know who lives there now!' Spike told the
others. 'It's a very old man. He stared at me and Spot
before going indoors.'

The gang had planned to meet at the house as usual on
Saturday morning and investigate further, but something
happened which changed their lives for a while. When Joe
and Matt awoke that morning, it was to find their father
sitting in the kitchen, looking very worried.

'Mum's not at all well today—she has a lot of pain in her

stomach,' he told the boys. 'The doctor's on his way. Can you get your own breakfasts and tidy up afterwards? Try to be quiet so that your mum can sleep.'

'Yes, Dad, of course we will,' said Joe. He and Matt were shocked. They could not remember their mum ever being ill or staying in bed. They looked at each other and didn't quite know what to say.

'I'll set the table,' said Matt.

'And I'll put the kettle on to make some tea,' responded Joe. They had just started when the doorbell rang. Both boys ran to open it, but their dad had arrived first. It was the doctor. He went upstairs with their father and stayed there for a long time, or so it seemed to the boys. They tried to eat their breakfasts, but they found they had no appetite. Eventually they heard footsteps and heard their dad let the doctor out. Then he came into the kitchen, and he looked very tired and was obviously upset.

'The doctor has phoned for an ambulance to come,' he said. 'I'm afraid that Mum has to go into hospital at once. She needs an operation straight away. I must go with her. That means leaving you on your own. I'll tell you as soon as I can what's happening.'

Joe could see that Matt was crumbling and he knew he had to be strong and try to take charge.

'All right, Dad,' he said. 'Don't worry about us at all. I'll take care of Matt. Let me pour you a cup of tea. Do you want a piece of toast? You'd better have something before you go to the hospital.'

In spite of everything, Joe's dad had to smile. Joe was so like his mother: very thoughtful and responsible.

'I may be gone for some time. Could you ring Mrs Fraser

and see if she could keep an eye on you two until I get back? And, yes, I will have that cup of tea and some toast after I've got a bag ready for your mum to take with her.'

Joe went to the phone and rang Spike's house, asking to speak to his mum. She quickly came to the phone and told Joe that she would come round straight away to help in whatever way she could.

Within a few minutes Mrs Fraser had arrived. She went straight upstairs to see the boys' mum. Then the boys crept upstairs too to see their mother before she went to hospital.

Matt was struggling not to cry when he saw how pale his mother looked. She smiled at him. 'I'll be all right, don't worry,' she said. 'Just be good and helpful until I get home. Mrs Fraser suggests you go round to their house for meals and just come home to sleep. It's so kind of her!'

'We promise that we won't be any trouble,' Matt said. 'Please get well quickly!'

'We'll come to see you as often as we can,' said Joe, 'and don't you worry about us—we're big now, and we'll do all we can to help Dad.'

'I know you will,' she replied.

The doorbell rang again and the ambulancemen appeared. As the boys saw their mother carried by stretcher into the ambulance, they felt very alone and, suddenly, not so very grown up!

Mrs Fraser put an arm around each of the boys.

'Have you eaten?' she asked.

'We did try, but didn't feel very hungry,' answered Matt.

'Well, I think the best thing is for you to tidy the kitchen while I tidy your mum's bedroom, then we'll go round to my house. Your dad will phone as soon as he can.

If you've got any homework, bring that with you. It's best that we all stay together and keep one another company,' she said in her usual cheery voice.

It seemed a very long morning but Joe and Matt were glad to be at Spike's house. They tried to do some homework, but found it hard to concentrate, so they ended up playing a computer game with Spike and Sally. It was almost lunch-time before the call came from the hospital.

'I'm sorry it's been so long,' said Dad, 'but Mum's been having lots of tests. She's now going to the operating theatre. I'm afraid you won't be able to see her today. I'll ring later.'

'All right, Dad.' Joe was trying to be brave. 'We'll be fine here. Please give our love to Mum.' Joe found his legs were shaking as he put the phone down.

He went into the kitchen to find Spike's mum. She had always been like a second mum to him and Matt.

'Aunty Jane,' he said, calling her by the name they had used when they were small children. Somehow, he wanted her to be his 'aunty' again.

'Aunty Jane, I know we don't go to church like you do, but if we talked to God and prayed for our mum, would he listen?'

Mrs Fraser could hear the desperation in the boy's voice. She silently asked God to give her the right words to help Joe.

'Of course God will listen, Joe. He loves us all so much, whether or not we go to church. Let's sit down right now and talk to him,' she said.

Then she took Joe's hands in hers and spoke a prayer, quietly asking God to be very near Joe and Matt's parents and also the surgeon and the nurses. She asked that all would go well and that soon their mother would be able to come home again. At the end of the prayer, Joe added his own words: 'Please, God, I don't know much about you, but I want to learn more. That's why I've started going to church with Spike. Please heal my mum. Amen.'

After talking to God in this way, Joe felt relieved. Ever since he had woken up and discovered that his mother was ill, he had felt a weight like a big stone on his heart and his mouth had felt dry. But after praying, the weight had gone. He smiled at Mrs Fraser and she smiled back. It was as if she knew what he felt. She gave him a hug.

'Now, Joe,' she said, 'can you please set the table for me, as lunch is nearly ready.' Joe was glad he had something to do.

All thoughts of the gang meeting that day were forgotten. The four children did take Spot for a short walk, but the rest of the time they stayed indoors and near the phone in case there was any more news. It seemed to Matt and Joe that it was the longest day they had ever known.

When their father arrived in the evening to collect them, he looked very tired and worried. He sat the boys down and told them about their mother.

'The operation has gone well,' he said, 'but the surgeon found that she had a huge tumour in her stomach. He hopes that he has managed to take it all away, but it's too early to tell yet. She will need lots of rest. It may take a long time for her to get better.'

'Has she got cancer?' Matt asked, hardly daring to look at his father's face. He hated to ask, but he needed to know.

'The tumour will be sent away to the laboratory for examination,' said Dad. 'Nobody can be 100 per cent sure at this stage, but it could be cancer. However, we must all be brave for Mum's sake. Even if it is cancer, there is a very good chance of a complete recovery.

'Joe, you're very quiet,' he added, turning to his elder son. He knew his older boy was very thoughtful and kept turning things over in his mind. He didn't want him to be worrying all night.

'Well, Dad,' Joe answered, 'after you phoned and told us about the operation, I went to Aunty Jane in the kitchen and we said a prayer together for God to heal Mum, and somehow, deep down, I just feel that she will be all right.'

'That's great, son,' his dad answered. 'You keep believing and praying. The Frasers are very good friends and I am happy if you learn to pray.'

'Are you going to church with Spike tomorrow?' Matt asked Joe. 'If you are, then can I come too? I'd like to see the drum-kit they use.'

'Sure,' replied Joe, 'it'll be cool if you come. Spike will be pleased.'

'Well, then,' said their dad, 'that's fixed. You two go to church in the morning and I'll go to the hospital. If Mum is strong enough, I'll come and get you and you can visit in the afternoon. She'll be longing to see her boys!'

So began several weeks that were very difficult for the family. Joe and Matt's mother came home, but she took a long time to recover. The hospital reports were not good. She had cancer and no one could be sure that it had not spread to other parts of her body, so she needed to have a period of radiotherapy followed by chemotherapy. The boys had to grow up quickly and help out at home.

The deserted house was almost forgotten—but not quite. Spike was the one who kept an eye on it, walking past each day with Spot. He frequently saw the old man come out of his door and collect his milk, and they began to wave to each other.

Through those worrying weeks, Joe and Matt continued to go to the youth group at church with Spike each Sunday. Several times Joe spoke to the leader and asked questions because he really wanted to find out what it meant to be a Christian. He was also asking God each day for his mother to be healed.

Matt enjoyed the band at the church and was really excited when the drummer offered to give him lessons. After church was finished, he stayed behind for half an hour, and it was the best half-hour of his week! He had to admit that church wasn't as boring as he had thought!

Chapter ten

Everyone was glad when the summer holidays arrived. Joe and Matt's mother had finished her course of radiotherapy and, although she was still weak, she looked and felt better. She was beginning to be able to do more things around the house, although the boys still did all they could to help her.

From the end of July to the beginning of August, the weather was warm and sunny, so once they had done their jobs at home, Matt and Joe were free to go out with Spike. There was only one major item on their agenda: a Whistler gang meeting in their den! They had talked from time to time about the deserted house, and Joe had written up all their findings and theories very neatly in a new notebook.

As they hadn't been there for such a long time, they decided to take the football and kick it over the fence in the way they had done on their first visits. They practised their whistles and felt very confident as they set off together down The Drive. Joe had his mobile with him in case his mother needed anything, but she wanted the boys to go out and have some fun together.

As planned, Spike kicked the football into the garden. Then Joe went through the gate and pretended to look for the ball, before whistling for the others.

There had been no sign of the old man next door, so the boys quickly went to the back of the house and one by one climbed through the window. Nothing had changed since their last visit. The boys stocked up the cupboard with snacks, and put cans of drink on the shelves.

They went into the kitchen, sat down and talked about the house.

'I think we should go to the spare room and search the drawers and wardrobe,' suggested Matt.

'OK,' agreed Joe, 'but let's be very careful not to disturb those fingerprints we saw. It's such a funny thing that they're there; they may be important for some reason.'

The boys trooped upstairs. The tarpaulin that covered the hole in the wall where the extension was being built was even more torn. Matt wanted to try to climb out and have a look at the building.

'No!' Spike said firmly to Matt. 'If you climb up there, anybody can see you.'

'And it may be really unsafe,' added Joe. 'If you fell, what would I say to Mum and Dad? I'm the eldest and supposed to be responsible. Mum has enough worry without adding any more!' declared Joe.

'I suppose you're both right, but we might have found some clues there,' said Matt reluctantly.

'Let's see if we can find any more indoors,' said Spike, as they went into the guest-room.

It was just as they had left it. The fingerprints were still on the chest of drawers, covered with a fine layer of dust. Joe carefully started to open the drawers without touching the top of the chest. He was disappointed to find that they were all completely empty. Then Spike went to the wardrobe. All the hanging space was empty, but on the floor there was a large, shallow cardboard box with a lid.

'What's this?' asked Spike. Matt pulled it onto the bed and took off the lid. Dust flew everywhere and Joe began to cough.

The box was full of old papers and maps. At first, it didn't look very interesting and Spike was about to close it up.

'Wait!' said Joe. 'Let's look at the maps.'

They pulled them out and saw that they were of Africa. Joe didn't recognize all the names of the countries.

'These maps are old,' he said. 'The names of the countries have all changed, but this map seems to be of Central Africa. Look, some of these areas have been marked. This seems to be a mountain range. The writing is pretty faint, but I think it says ... something ... "volcanoes"!'

Joe was getting excited, and the other two peered over the map to see.

'There are letters here as well,' commented Spike, pulling some more paper out from the box. 'These are old too, and almost falling to pieces!'

'Take great care as you handle them,' advised Joe. 'Spread them out on the bed.'

Matt began to try to read the letter at the top of the pile. The ink had faded a lot, but he managed to make out most of what it said. It went something like this:

'My dear Paul,

'I am writing to you from Rwanda. We have been exploring the Virunga Volcanoes, but it is very difficult terrain. As well as having to trek through thick bamboo forest, there is the danger of being attacked by the mountain gorillas. They wander freely through these forests between Uganda, Belgian Congo and Ruanda-Urundi. They know no borders, and we never know where they are. The largest males are called silver backs, and they are very fierce. We heard one roaring not far from our camp yesterday. I can tell you, it was a scary sound!

'All of our party have been sick with malaria and backwater fever. The latter is a killer, and sadly we had to dig a grave for Sidney and bury him on the same day that he died. It was a terrible day for us. Then I had to write to his widow. A native took the letter to Kigali for me to send to England.

'Our survey of the flora of these mountains is almost finished. We hope soon to return to England. There is one extra task I have been asked to do, and it is secret for now, but it involves crossing again into the Congo. It is risky, and part of me wishes I had not agreed to undertake it. If I do not arrive home by the end of the year, send a search party out for me. Get them to start at Goma and head for Matshimbi. For now, keep all this "under your hat". If my mission succeeds, it will restore our family fortunes.

'Now I must finish. Tonight a native runner whom I can trust will take this letter to Kigali to the post.

*'How is your little treasure? Give him a big hug
from his great-uncle! Take care of yourself and your
pretty wife.*
  'Your ever-loving uncle,
  'Samuel Jenkins.'

The boys were excited to find all this information.
'Do you think his uncle came back?' asked Matt. 'And
do you think his "little treasure" was the boy who had the
bedroom here?'

'You mean the one who died?' replied Joe.

'We don't know for sure that he did die, we just guessed
he did,' Spike corrected Joe.

'Maybe the uncle never came back, and Paul and
his wife went to find him and also didn't come back!'
suggested Matt.

'That's a possibility,' said Joe. 'Let's leave the papers on
the bed for now and go downstairs for a drink. This dust is
really making me wheeze!'

Back in the kitchen the boys talked over the letter
and how it linked with the mystery. Joe wrote about it in
the notebook.

'When we get home,' suggested Spike, 'let's try to look
up Samuel Jenkins on the Internet and see if we can find
out if he was an explorer or something like that.'

'Brilliant!' said Joe. 'It's lunch-time now anyway,
so we'll go home. We can come again very soon,
maybe tomorrow.'

After lunch they met up again at Spike's home. They
put 'Samuel Jenkins' into the computer search engine.
The results were amazing! Samuel was a botanist and

had been sent on an expedition from the Royal Botanical
Gardens at Kew, London, in 1968 to Central Africa to find
plants in that area. He never returned from the expedition
and it was presumed he died from malaria, as others on
the expedition had done. In January 1971 a search party
returned, having been unable to find any survivors.

'It all makes sense now,' said Joe.

'What does?' asked Matt.

'Well, the plants in the garden, like the mimosa,'
explained Joe. 'It's a bit like a jigsaw puzzle, trying to fit
the pieces together!'

Chapter eleven

T he next morning Spike took Spot out as usual. He always did the same walk now, so that he could stop at the end of The Drive and look at the deserted house; often he would wave cheerfully to the old man when he brought in his milk. Today he waved as usual to the bent old man. The man immediately tried to straighten himself up and urgently beckoned Spike over. Spike felt a bit scared.

Spike crossed over the road and greeted him. Spot was at his heels, and it comforted Spike to know he was there. He knew they were trespassing when they went into the deserted house, and he wondered if they had been found out.

'I'm Tubby Tibbs,' said the man, struggling to say each word. He was breathless, and his lips had a bluish tinge. 'Not Tubby now, but used to be,' he added. 'I badly need help. I can't breathe. Can you get Dr Watts from the surgery to call?'

'Yes, sir,' answered Spike, so relieved that it was nothing to do with him being seen next door. 'I'll run straight home and get my mum to call him.' Then he thought quickly. 'Leave the door on the latch, so that he can get in. Shall I leave Spot to guard you?'

'Thanks, son,' Mr Tibbs said. So Spike told Spot to 'stay', and he obediently sat on the doorstep while Spike ran home as fast as he could.

'What's happened? Where's Spot?' asked Mrs Fraser, as Spike came running in. He told her about old Mr Tibbs, and she phoned the doctor's surgery straight away.

'I'd better go there at once,' she said. 'You stay here with Sally. I've got my mobile so I'll let you know what's happening.'

Mrs Fraser started to run down The Drive to find Spot waiting on the doorstep of Mr Tibbs's house, guarding a very sick man.

A bit later, Joe and Matt called for Spike. He told them all about Tubby Tibbs.

'We'd better not go near the house today,' said Joe. 'If doctors are calling next door, we shall have to be extra careful.'

'We'll see what Mum tells us when she gets back,' said Spike. 'It's such a shame—happening just as we seemed to be getting to the bottom of this mystery!' he grumbled.

'Maybe, if we get to know this old man, then he can tell us the history of the house,' said Matt. 'If he's so old, I expect he's lived in that house for ages.'

The boys decided to play a game of Monopoly with Sally, so they had to stop talking about the mystery. Soon Mrs Fraser returned with Spot at her heels.

'The poor old man has been taken into hospital,' she told the young people. 'He was so glad for your help, Spike. He's ninety-eight years old! I'll go to the hospital later on and visit.'

'Maybe I'll come with you,' suggested Spike, much to his mother's surprise.

'I'm sure he would appreciate that,' she responded.

After finishing their game the gang decided to go to their den now that the coast was clear.

Once inside, they rushed up to the guest bedroom to see what else might be in the cardboard box. Everything was laid out on the bed, just as they had left it.

Underneath the maps and letter was a piece of tissue paper which was folded in two. Inside it were a few pressed leaves, now looking very grey and brittle. The boys only looked at them; they didn't touch them.

'I think they must be some specimens from Africa,' remarked Joe. 'We mustn't break them.'

At the bottom of the box was a piece of paper. Joe took it out. It was odd: it had a few words on it, followed by a lot of numbers.

'Whatever is this?' asked Matt. 'It doesn't make sense!'

The paper had these words on it:

'I may not get home to give you your Christmas present.'

These were the numbers that followed:

*'20 4 4 13 / 5 16 8 / 25 2 1 / 20 11 5 14 14 / 9 3 16 8
? 17 4 19 11 5 17 20 / 2 16 / 6 2 24 3 16 10 / 8 5 25
22 3 20 3 21 / 21 11 4 / 21 11 19 2 16 4 / 2 16 / 23 11 3
7 11 / 16 2 / 13 3 16 10 / 11 5 20 / 20 5 21
3 16 10 5 11 2'*

The boys pored over the sheet of paper for a while.

'It must be a code!' said Spike. 'Joe, write down the numbers and let's see if we can work it out.'

'I wonder why it's in code? I thought that was the sort of thing they did in the war or in stories, but not in real life!' commented Joe.

He carefully copied down the numbers into his notebook.

'Shall Matt and I try to unravel it this afternoon while you visit the hospital, or shall we wait until this evening?'

'I don't mind,' said Spike. 'I offered to go with Mum because I thought that if I got to know Mr Tibbs, I might learn something about the house.'

'What do we do now?' Matt asked. 'Shall we put everything away?'

'Yes, I think so,' answered Joe. 'We could put the box in our cupboard downstairs. It's easier then if we want to look at the things—we can do so on the kitchen table.'

Back in the kitchen the boys discussed their discovery. It was mysterious and exciting. What did it mean? What was the house's secret?

'We'll work it out, however long it takes!' commented Joe.

'You know, we haven't really fully explored the lounge yet,' said Spike.

'I was thinking that too,' said Matt. 'But it's nearly dinner-time, and we need to check on Mum.'

Chapter twelve

That afternoon, Spike went to the hospital. He didn't often have time alone with his mother, time when they could talk, and Spike had been wanting to tell her about the night he asked Jesus into his life. There had never been the right opportunity, but as they travelled together, Spike realized that now was a good time.

'Mum,' said Spike, 'I want to tell you something. I've wanted to tell you it for a little while, from before Mrs Jones got so ill, but, well, I'm a bit stuck for words.'

Mrs Fraser gave her son her full attention.

'What is it, Spike? Are you in any kind of trouble?' she asked.

'No, it's nothing like that. In fact, you'll be pleased. I want to tell you that I've become a real Christian—inside, you know.' Spike fumbled to find the words to explain.

'That's wonderful! Thank you for telling me,' said his mum, giving Spike a huge smile. 'Can I tell Dad?'

'Of course, but it is sort of private, so you won't tell other people, will you?' Spike asked anxiously, because he didn't want all the old ladies at the church suddenly coming and hugging him or anything like that!

'Don't worry, love, it will be just our secret until you decide to tell anyone else.'

'Mum, I'm praying for Joe and Matt. I think God is answering, because they come to church with us.'

'They are great friends, Spike. Your dad and I are praying for all the Jones family.'

They arrived at the hospital and Spike felt so happy he had told his mother that he was a Christian. He didn't understand why it mattered so much, but it did.

They found Mr Tibbs looking very frail and small tucked up between the white sheets in the bed. Over his nose and mouth was an oxygen mask. He was dozing, but when they went over to him, he opened his eyes and smiled.

'How are you?' Mrs Fraser asked. 'Spike wanted to come and see you too.'

Mr Tibbs tried to pull off the mask and speak.

'Keep it on,' advised Mrs Fraser. 'We'll catch what you say.'

'Good boy,' Mr Tibbs struggled to speak, but pointed at Spike. 'Thank you.'

'That's all right,' Spike said, feeling a little uncomfortable.

'We brought you some things,' said Mrs Fraser, as she unpacked a bag with soap, a flannel and a towel. The old man smiled his gratitude.

'So kind,' he muttered.

They simply sat with him for a while, Mrs Fraser holding the old man's hand.

'I'll come again tomorrow,' she promised. Mr Tibbs looked directly at Spike and whispered through the mask, 'Come too.'

'I will,' promised Spike.

'He seems to have taken a liking to you, Spike,' said his mother as they walked out of the ward. Before they left she asked the sister about Mr Tibbs.

'He is very sick,' she explained. 'His heart is not working very well and he has a chest infection. The next twenty-four hours will be critical. He seems to be worried about paying the milkman and stopping his milk. He may have been rambling a bit because he is confused.'

'No,' said Spike, 'he gets a bottle of milk every day. I'll see the milkman early tomorrow morning and cancel it.'

While Spike was at the hospital, Joe and Matt were at home.

'I'm going to stay in with Mum this afternoon,' Joe told Matt. 'I can begin to try to crack that message we found.'

'OK,' replied Matt. 'I might go down to church for some drum practice. The music group are practising.'

'See you later, then!' said Joe. He put the kettle on to make his mother a cup of tea, and then took out his notebook.

'*20 4 4 13 / 5 16 8 / 25 2 1 / 20 11 5 14 14 / 9 3 16 8
? 17 4 19 11 5 17 20 / 2 16 / 6 2 24 3 16 10 / 8 5 25
22 3 20 3 21 / 21 11 4 / 21 11 19 2 16 4 / 2 16 / 23 11 3
7 11 / 16 2 / 13 3 16 10 / 11 5 20 / 20 5 21
3 16 10 5 11 2*'

Joe stared at the numbers. They seemed to make no sense at all. He deduced that there were four sentences, each word divided by a forward slash. That much was easy!

Joe liked doing puzzles and was good at them, but he

didn't know where to begin with this code.

Having sat and looked at it several times, he decided to make another cup of tea for his mother. She was resting upstairs and he carried it to her.

'Oh, Joe, thank you so much!' she said. 'Thank you for staying with me this afternoon. Sometimes it gets a bit lonely. What's Matt doing?'

'He's gone to church, Mum,' answered Joe. 'Steve, the drummer, is giving a lesson. I thought it would be all right for him to go.'

'Yes, that's fine. You two really like going to church, don't you?'

'Matt likes the band, but I've really learnt a lot about God,' said Joe shyly. 'I know that when I pray, God hears me, and I believe that you will one day be completely well.'

'Thank you, Joe. I'm glad you both go there. I want to ask you something. The leader of the youth group phoned last night, after you'd both gone to bed, and asked if you'd like to go on a week's camp, at the end of August. I promised to ask you. Dad has no objection. Would you like to go?'

'Oh, Mum, I'd love to, but you'll have to ask Matt. Is Spike going? He didn't say anything to us.'

'Your dad wants to treat Spike, as a way of saying "thank you" to Aunty Jane for all her help while I was in hospital. He planned to talk to the Frasers this evening, after I'd spoken to you. When Matt comes home, we'll see what he feels about it.'

Joe felt really pleased about the possibility of going to camp. They would need to solve the mystery, though, because the summer holidays would soon fly by!

He left his mother to rest and took the code to his room. The more he looked at it, the more disappointed he became, because he couldn't work it out. He wrote down all the letters of the alphabet and tried all sorts of sequences, but nothing made any sense.

Just as he was despairing and going to give it up and watch TV instead, Joe worked out that there were two two-letter words that must be opposites: '2 16' appeared in the second line and '16 2' in the fourth. Joe began to list all the two-letter words that could be written backwards as well as forwards. He thought of four words that worked that way: *oh* and *ho*, and *on* and *no*. *Oh* and *ho* didn't seem very likely, so he pencilled in 'on/no' in both places.

He then deduced that 16 must be either *n* or *o*, as must 2. Then he looked for all the other 2s and 16s, and pencilled above them 'n/o'. It was a start! Joe was very pleased with himself.

He heard Matt come in, humming to himself. Joe whistled to him in their code, 'Come up here!' Matt whistled back and went to Joe's room.

'How are you getting on, brain-box?' Matt asked his brother.

'It's very complicated, but I've deduced two letters—I'm just not sure which number means which letter.' Joe showed his brother what he had worked out, and Matt was duly impressed.

'Oh, Matt,' Joe said, remembering, 'the church youth leader rang Mum and Dad last night and asked if we'd like to go to camp for a week. I said I would. Would you?'

'Wouldn't mind,' said Matt. 'So long as there isn't too much God stuff. Is Spike going?'

'He doesn't know about it yet. Mum and Dad want to treat him as a "thank you" to Aunty Jane for helping us so much when Mum was ill. It would give Mum a real rest if we were away for that week too,' he added.

'I'll go and tell Mum I'd like to go,' said Matt.

So the two boys settled that the Whistlers would all go to the youth camp.

Chapter thirteen

The next morning the boys met at Spike's house. They went to his room and sat on his bed, trying to puzzle out a bit more of the code. It was Spike who had the idea of working out which number occurred most frequently. The number 5 seemed to crop up quite a lot, as did 20. They were getting nowhere fast when Matt suddenly had an idea.

'Look at the low numbers,' he said. 'They come quite often. If we take the 2 as *o*, maybe all the other low numbers are vowels. That would mean that the 5 which occurs frequently is a vowel.'

'But if they are vowels, then *o* would be 4,' objected Spike. The boys sat and thought about this. Matt was sure he had sussed the vowels out.

'Got it!' he shouted in excitement. 'The numbers run backwards! *A* is 5, *e* is 4, and so on.'

'Wow! Well done!' Joe was as excited as his brother. 'On that basis, let's pencil the vowels in.'

Working on the same basis, they were then able to fit in 16 as *n*. Suddenly they cracked the code. All the other numbers went forwards once the 1–5 for vowels had been taken out! They very excitedly worked out the message:

'SEEK AND YOU SHALL FIND.
?PERHAPS ON BOXING DAY
VISIT THE THRONE ON WHICH NO KING
HAS SAT
INGAHO'

'But it doesn't make any sense!' said Matt,
very disappointed.

'It's a cryptic message,' said Joe.

'What does "cryptic" mean?' asked Spike.

'Well,' said Joe, 'it's another sort of coded message. You
have to look at the clues and try to work out what they
mean. It's like doing a treasure hunt.'

The boys set off to the deserted house to find more
clues. It seemed strange to Spike not to be looking for old
Mr Tibbs, and he couldn't help thinking about him. He
was looking forward to visiting him again. When they were
safely inside the house, Spike told the others that Mr Tibbs
had been too sick to talk to him.

The boys agreed to explore the lounge because they had
not yet done this in detail. The sun was pouring through a
large French window that opened onto a patio in the back
garden. The sunlight seemed to show up all the dust on
the furniture. On one wall were more bookcases, which
contained books on botany, a large atlas and several books
about foreign countries. Each side of the fireplace there
were glass-fronted cabinets, then shelves, beneath which
were more cupboards.

The boys looked at the glass-fronted cabinets. They
displayed all sorts of interesting items. Some were easily
recognizable, like African carvings and Indian brass;

others were just pretty ornaments. But there were also some rather strange objects which none of them liked. They made Spike feel very uncomfortable. He had a strong notion that God didn't like them very much either, because they were evil. He warned Joe and Matt, 'I don't think we should touch those things. I think they're evil.'

'What do you mean?' asked Matt. 'They just look a bit odd: bones and dried skin and shells.'

'I can't say exactly, but they're sending shivers down my spine, and I think they are used in witchcraft!' Spike answered.

'Well,' said Joe, 'I'll just record what they look like; we won't touch them.'

Joe went to have a closer look and he noticed that there were fingerprints near the objects, just like those Spike had found in the guest-room.

'Look here!' he said. 'Someone has touched these things since the house was deserted!' In his notebook he carefully made notes about all that they had observed.

The cupboards beneath the shelves seemed to have once been a home for mice! There was chewed-up paper, jigsaw puzzles and card games. A teddy bear fell out of one cupboard. One of its ears had been chewed, and stuffing fell out.

'Let's shut the door and leave it to the mice!' said Matt. He had seen enough!

'I think Matt's right,' said Joe. He walked over to the French windows. 'Look! Even though the garden is so overgrown, you can just see Mr Tibbs's house from here. I wonder if he saw the person who left the fingerprints?'

The three boys retreated to the kitchen.

'I've been thinking,' said Matt. 'We got into this house easily and made it our den. I think we should take the cardboard box home to keep it safe. If we could get in and find it, so could other people, too. We decoded the message, but we don't want to risk anyone else doing that, do we?'

'Good thinking,' said Spike. 'But wouldn't it be stealing if we did that? I really don't want to be a thief.'

'Why don't we just take the letters?' suggested Matt. 'They're the biggest clues.'

'Good thinking, Matt,' said Joe. 'Let's put the box back in the wardrobe.'

Spike fetched the box and carefully took out the letters, replacing the box just where they had found it before they all went home.

After lunch Spike went with his mother back to the hospital. He was delighted to see Mr Tibbs sitting up and looking better.

'I'm really grateful to you, lad,' said Mr Tibbs. 'You saved my life!'

'I spoke to the milkman for you,' said Spike. 'I'll tell him when you come home.'

'It'll be a few days before I'm fighting fit again,' said Mr Tibbs, 'but I am so grateful to you both for helping me. Fine boy you have there, missus!'

Spike went red with embarrassment and was glad when his mother went to talk to the nurse. It left Spike alone with his new friend.

'Have you lived in that house for long, Mr Tibbs?' he asked politely.

'Now lad, Tubby's my name, like I told you. Well, I've lived there for seventy-five years. My wife, Mabel, and I were newly wed. Yes, I've lived in that house most of my long life and ever since it was built.'

Spike took a deep breath. Maybe it was now or never.

'What about the next-door house?' he tried to ask in as normal a voice as he could.

'Oh, lad!' Tubby looked hard at Spike. 'I know you go there with your two pals. Don't fret now,' he added, as Spike began to look anxious, 'I won't tell on you. Just be careful, 'tis a very bad place, that house.'

Spike took another breath to ask why, but at that moment he heard the ward door swing open and his mother's footsteps.

'Thanks, Tubby,' was all he managed to say. 'You're a real mate. I'll visit you when you get home. I'll bring Spot.'

'I'd like that—I'd like that very much,' the old man said.

'Sister says you're doing well,' said Mrs Fraser. 'Hopefully you won't have to stay here too long. We have to go now,' she added.

They said their goodbyes and started on the way home.

'By the way, Spike,' said his mother, 'would you like to go to the church youth camp that's coming up soon?'

'You bet! Can I really?'

'Yes. The Joneses want to treat you to it as a way of saying "thank you" for our help when Aunty Linda was in hospital. Joe and Matt have already said that they're going.'

'Wow, that's so exciting!' said Spike. 'I prayed about it, but I didn't want to ask you. I thought that if we could all go, it might help Joe and Matt to become Christians. Last term I was bullied at school for going to the CU and Joe stood up for me. After that he started to come to church.'

'I'd forgotten that Joe helped you then!' said his mother. 'That was really kind of him.'

'Yes, Joe stood up for me,' Spike replied. 'Because he's older and also a prefect, they took notice of him and have never troubled me since. Actually, that was the first time I prayed—well, really prayed—you know what I mean!'

'Yes, I know,' replied his mother. 'When we cry out to God because we need him to help, he always hears us!'

'I can't wait to get home and talk about camp with Matt and Joe!' said Spike.

Chapter fourteen

That evening the Whistlers met in Joe's bedroom. They were all excited about camp. They discussed the various activities which they had been told they could do.

After discussing camp, Spike told the others about Tubby.

'We need to talk together because he knows about us,' Spike explained. 'He's watched us go in and out but hasn't grassed on us. I didn't have much time to talk, but he has lived next door ever since the houses were built. I know he knows something. He said it was a "bad place". I couldn't ask him what he meant because Mum came back just then. I want to see him again. He's a great old man.

'Anyway, before I go home, can we look at the message again?' Spike added.

'Good idea,' responded Matt. 'We need all our brains to work it out!'

'"Seek and you shall find,"' read Joe. 'That seems pretty straightforward. I've heard those words before. Is it a quotation from a book?'

'It's from the Bible,' Spike answered. 'Jesus said those words. He said, "Ask and it will be given to you; seek and you will find; knock and the door will be opened to you.''

'Did Jesus really say that?' asked Joe. 'Those are pretty cool things to promise!'

'I think it's about praying. If you want something and mean it with all your heart, then ask God, and, if it's according to his will and if it will help show his greatness, he promises your answer.'

'I know it's nothing to do with our mystery, but when Mum was so ill with cancer, I prayed with all my heart that she would recover. Ever since, I've felt sure that she will be all right. I know God heard my prayer.'

'Do you think it would be all right to ask God about us finding the meaning of the message, or do you think he's too big to be interested in our mystery?' asked Matt.

'Well, it's not as important as your mum getting well, but we could try,' said Spike.

The room went very quiet. No one wanted to speak first.

'It was your idea, Matt, so why don't you pray?' said Joe.

'I've never done it—I don't know how,' confessed Matt.

'It's easy! You just talk to God as you would your dad,' said Spike. 'But as we all want to ask him, why don't we all do it together, after a count of three: one, two, three ...'

The boys all began at once, asking God to help them understand the message.

'Well, let's look at what we already know,' said Joe. 'We have to look for something—maybe in a religious place, a church, or somewhere where there is a Bible.'

He wrote it down in his notebook.

'"? perhaps on Boxing Day"—what does that mean?'

'Perhaps it means it is a Christmas present that has been hidden,' suggested Matt.

'The other letter talked about a secret and risky task and said, "send out a search party if I'm not back by the end of the year", so perhaps this is to do with that. Boxing Day is the day after Christmas Day.' Joe was thinking aloud.

'Could be,' said Spike. 'Or, perhaps the thing we're looking for is hidden in a box. Well, we did find the message in a box.'

Joe was busy writing everyone's thoughts down when there was a tap at his bedroom door.

'Hi boys!' It was Matt and Joe's dad. 'Time for supper!' The meeting was adjourned.

That night, before bed, Spike asked his father about Boxing Day. He wanted to know the origin of the name. His dad told him that he thought the name came from servants receiving boxes of gifts from their masters, but that the day was, in fact, St Stephen's Day.

Mr Fraser told his son, 'Remember the carol "Good King Wenceslas"? He looked out on the feast of Stephen, and that is December 26th. Why do you want to know, anyway? It seems an odd thing to ask about in August!'

Spike laughed. 'Well, you know me, I'm always getting muddled! It was just something I was thinking about. Thanks, Dad, you've answered my question.'

Mr Fraser looked at his son and laughed too. 'Time for bed, son,' he said. 'I think you have a dog to take for a walk in the morning.'

Spike was excited. He might have solved the next clue: perhaps they had to look in a St Stephen's church.

The next day, Spike wanted to visit Mr Tibbs. He told his mother that Joe and Matt might go with him. His

mother made him promise not to wear the old man out.
So Spike sent a text message to Joe to suggest they caught
the 2 p.m. bus to the hospital. They arranged to meet up
after lunch.

Spike was pleased. He wanted Tubby to meet the others.

'Hi, Tubby, how are you doing?' asked Spike, as the boys
greeted the old man.

'Just fine, my son, just fine,' replied Mr Tibbs.

'These are my friends, Joe and Matt Jones,' said Spike
as he introduced them. 'We're the Whistlers gang.'

'I guessed you must be!' said Tubby. 'I've seen you going
next door and heard your whistles. Very good too, if I may
say so! We used to do things like that when I was young.
We had gangs and dens and secret signs. Your secret is safe
with me, but be careful!'

'When you said that it was a bad house, what exactly did
you mean?' asked Spike.

'Well, it has a history does that house. It's full of bad
luck. I worry a bit about you when you're in there. Never
try to get out onto that extension, will you!' he said
very gravely.

'Can you tell us why the house was deserted?' asked Joe.

Tubby looked at Joe. He took a deep breath.

'It's a long story. I moved into The Drive when the
houses were first built, with my Mabel. The house next
door was bought by a nice couple, Mr and Mrs Tanner.
They had two children, a boy and a girl. Mabel loved those
children! Danny and Sarah became like our own, running
in and out the house. Then, one day, their mum became ill.
It was the days when you had to pay the doctor to visit, and
before antibiotics were in common use. Mrs Tanner became

worse and died. That's when the sadness descended on the house, and from that time it has never left.

'Before long, Mr Tanner knocked on our door and told us he couldn't keep up the payments on the house. The family moved away. That was in the war.'

'Who bought the house next?' Matt asked. He wanted to hear more.

'Well, it lay empty for a while. No one had money during the war. Then the council used it to house a family who had been bombed out.'

Tubby began to cough, and Spike remembered that his mother had said they must not tire the old man.

'I think we should leave you to rest,' he said, 'but if we may, can we visit you again tomorrow and hear some more?'

'Please do,' said Tubby, 'you've cheered me up good and proper!'

They all said goodbye and went to catch the bus back home.

'He's great!' said Joe. 'I need to go straight home and write down what he's told us. It may be important!'

'Oh, I forgot to tell you,' Spike said. 'I was asking my dad last night what Boxing Day meant, and he told me that Boxing Day has another name: St Stephen's Day. You know, Good King Wenceslas and all that about the feast of Stephen? So our clue could be to find a church called St Stephen's!'

'Well done!' said Joe. 'I think you're on to something there!'

'Maybe God did hear and answer the prayers we asked last night,' commented Matt.

Chapter fifteen

The next day, the boys wanted to see Tubby again. They almost ran into the ward!

'You're so kind to come again,' he said. 'I hoped you would, but didn't dare count on it. I know young men have all sorts of important things to do with their time!

'Now, I must tell you some good news: the doctor will let me go home tomorrow! Spike, could you make sure the milkman leaves me some milk, please?'

'No problem,' responded Spike. 'Spot and I will do that in the morning.'

'Now, Whistlers, I have to speak to you very seriously,' continued old Mr Tibbs. 'So far you've been pretty safe going in and out of next door. However, if I now have to have visits from nurses and doctors, you may not be quite so safe. I think it might be best if you call at my house first, and then, if the coast is clear, you can go out of my back garden and over the fence into the house. When you leave, you'll have to take great care if you don't want your den to be discovered.'

The three boys looked at one another and agreed that it was a good plan.

'Thank you, Tubby,' said Joe, 'it's very kind of you to keep our secret. We haven't damaged anything in the house, and we promise not to do so.'

'Well, I guess you want to hear more about that house,' said Mr Tibbs, smiling at the boys. 'I think we'd got to the war. Well, eventually a buyer came along and the house was sold. He was a middle-aged bachelor and pretty well kept himself to himself. His name was Mr Jenkins. I think his first name was Samuel.'

The boys looked at one another with delight. They had come across that name before!

'He was a lonely sort of soul was Mr Jenkins,' continued Tubby. 'He never talked much to us. He did come round sometimes to tell us that he was going to be away for a while. He was very clever, a botanist working up at Kew Gardens, if I remember rightly, and he used to go round the world finding plants.'

'Did he own the Land Rover?' asked Matt.

'No, son,' answered Mr Tibbs, 'that comes later in the story.

'Mr Jenkins spoke with a very posh accent, and he told my Mabel that he was brought up in a big country house, but that his family had lost everything in the Great Depression.

'Well, one day, Mr Jenkins came round to us with his key,' continued Mr Tibbs.

'"I'm off on my travels again,"' he said, "But my nephew, Paul Jenkins, will be coming to live here. He's getting married, and he and his bride will make it their home. I expect to be away for four months in South America."

'Anyway, a few weeks later, there's a knock at the
door and we see this pretty girl and a young man. They
introduced themselves as Lucy and Paul Jenkins, so we
reckoned they were our new neighbours. As we got to know
them we learned a bit of their story. Lucy was from gypsy
stock. She was very dark-haired and pretty. Her family was
not at all happy when she wanted to marry out of the gypsy
clan. His family was equally appalled at their son running
off with a gypsy girl! They cut him off without a penny. Not
that the family had many pennies left, as I understand it!
That was when Paul's uncle, Samuel Jenkins, offered them
his home. He had always been fond of his nephew, and he
thought it very romantic when Paul ran off and married a
gypsy girl!'

Mr Tibbs lay back on his pillows.

'Are you all right, Tubby?' asked Spike. 'We don't want
to tire you out!'

'I'll just tell you a bit more now,' Mr Tibbs answered. 'I
want you to know why it is a bad house.

'Well, Paul worked away most of the week at a big
country estate. That's why he had a Land Rover. Lucy
seemed happy enough. Often she came in to talk to Mabel.
She was restless, and not used to living in a house and
staying in one place. But she was a sweet girl, and very
much in love.

'One day she told Mabel that she was "expecting"! We
were thrilled for the couple. Just before the baby was born,
Mr Jenkins came back from his long expedition. He, too,
was very excited at the thought of a baby in the house.
Christmas came, and at the turn of the year, little Samuel
was born! Mr Jenkins doted on him like a granddad! He

kept telling Paul and Lucy to have lots more children and fill the house with the sound of little feet! It was his suggestion that they build a few more rooms. He wanted to live in the house with Paul and Lucy and see little Sam grow up, but then he was asked to go out to Africa, collecting plants again.

'When Sam was about two and a half, Lucy was "expecting" again. The midwife thought she had twins on the way. Paul was still working away all through the week. It was a struggle for Lucy. Young Sam was quite a handful, and she was always tired.

'One terrible day, Lucy fell asleep for a few minutes. The builders had knocked a hole through into the house from the extension, to make a doorway. Young Sam, tired of playing with his toys, toddled off to see what the men were doing. They were having a tea-break and a fag, and no one was around to watch young Sam. He fell to his death!

'It was so terrible! The scream and then the silence! Poor Lucy, it broke her heart! The shock was too much. She started to miscarry and lost the twins. She almost lost her mind, too! She needed her family, but the Romany people have their own superstitions and said that she and the house were cursed and they wouldn't come near her. In the end, she just ran away. Without his sweetheart, Paul couldn't cope. Even though his uncle was due home for Christmas (he'd wanted to be around for little Sam's third birthday), Paul couldn't stay in the house.

'He told the builders to go and paid them as if they'd finished the job. He never wanted to see them again. He left everything and went off with a backpack. Neither he nor his uncle ever returned. The house remains the property of Paul and Lucy, for his uncle had made it over to them. Perhaps one day, one of them will return.'

Having finished his story, Tubby lay back on the pillows, and Spike noticed a tear trickle down his face.

'I'm so sorry, Tubby, so very sorry. I'm sorry if we've upset you, making you remember it,' he said.

'It's all right, son, don't fret for me,' Mr Tibbs replied. 'My life's nearly over, and I've seen much sadness. But that is a bad house. I would like to see it pulled down!'

The three boys were very sad at what they had heard. It made the things they had seen and found fit into place like pieces of a jigsaw.

'Now, boys, cheer up! It all happened a long time ago,' said Mr Tibbs. 'Come and see me when I'm back home, and I'll teach you some new bird whistles if I have enough breath. I used to be good at those!'

It was time to go anyway. The boys said goodbye to Tubby and walked quietly out of the ward, still rather shocked and sad at what they had learnt.

'It all makes sense now, doesn't it?' said Matt to the others.

'Yes,' said Joe. 'But somehow it seems even more important now that we find out the meaning of the message.'

Chapter sixteen

Once Mr Tibbs came home, his whole life changed for the better, with daily visits from the boys, Spot and often Mrs Fraser. They all kept a good eye on him.

As he had promised, Tubby began to teach the boys some new whistles. He knew lots of bird-calls, and the boys were quick to learn. They decided to wait until after camp before they talked to him again about the house. They hoped that by that time there would be fewer people going to visit him and it would be safer for them to go back to their den. Spike certainly didn't want his mother or his little sister to discover their secret den.

The days went quickly, and soon it was time for the boys to go to camp. They were given a kit list, so even packing was fun. Nineteen youngsters were going to the camp, and they already knew one another pretty well.

The day they travelled was lovely and sunny. The first thing everyone wanted to do when they arrived was have a dip in the nearby sea!

Joe was in a different tent from Spike and Matt. The other three boys in his tent—Adam, Mark and Jason—were all fourteen. Jason went to Veritas High School like Joe, Matt and Spike.

They had a tent officer, a young man called Roy, whom Joe had never seen at the church. Joe found out that that was because Roy had been away for two years in Central Africa on a short-term teaching assignment. Joe made a mental note of this; maybe this guy knew something about Congo or Rwanda, and could help them with the message they were struggling with? Joe knew that he would have to ask Spike and Matt if he could tell Roy about it.

Matt and Spike were in a tent with twin brothers called Tim and Tom. They were already friends with the twins from the Sunday group. The two were fantastic at table-tennis; nobody in the youth group could beat them, not even the leaders! Matt and Spike sensed that camp would be fun! Their tent officer was Steve, already a friend as he was the one who had been teaching Matt the drums.

Each morning, the campers were woken by a whistle. Then, after everyone had finished breakfast, they returned to their tents to have a short time called 'devotions'. This was a completely new idea to Joe and Matt. At devotions, the boys read a passage from the Bible and had a chance to ask questions and discuss what they thought about it. Matt was very shy at first, but soon he joined in, as Spike and the twins had no inhibitions about asking questions.

'Whoever would have thought that reading the Bible could actually be interesting?' he thought to himself.

As the week progressed, Matt was pleased to be able to ask some of the questions which had been bothering him since his mother had been diagnosed with cancer. He had been worrying about death, and whether there was really a life afterwards. He hadn't dared ask anyone at home because they might think he was expecting his mum to die, and also because he couldn't face his own fears that she might. It became obvious to Matt that the other three in his group all seemed to know God and talked to him as a friend, and he felt distinctly different. This troubled him, as Spike had been his best friend all his life. He felt a bit jealous of Tim and Tom, as they shared a bond with Spike that he didn't have.

Joe was also finding the 'devotions' an interesting time. Over the past few months he had been thinking about the Christian faith. Twice he had felt that God had heard his prayers. Yet he was unsure if he was really a Christian. He loved his dad very much and looked up to him; he was a great guy, but he didn't go to church, read the Bible or pray. Wasn't he a Christian? Joe spent a lot of time in the tent devotions just thinking and quietly questioning. He liked Roy, and sometimes on their excursions he would try to walk with him and ask him more about Christianity. Joe was a guy who liked to think things out.

After the devotions, the teenagers were able to choose what they wanted to do. There were various options each day, all pretty energetic. Matt learnt to abseil down cliffs, Joe was able to do orienteering, and Spike often chose the water-sports option. Most days the weather was pretty good.

After supper the campers gathered together. If it was nice enough they lit a fire and sat around it on logs. They sang songs, sometimes camp-fire songs such as the Scouts and Guides sang, and sometimes Christian ones. Steve was the leader of this part of the proceedings, and everyone

seemed to enjoy it. After the singing, the camp leader,
James, or his wife, Sue, would give a short talk telling the
campers more about who Jesus was and what he did when
he died on the cross.

As the week drew to a close, Joe knew that he didn't
want camp to end! He loved it! He knew, too, that he
wanted to be a Christian. He felt that he could trust Roy
and could talk to him. He was wondering how he could get
alone with him.

On their last day, all the campers went for a hike.
Without really thinking about it, the Whistlers began to
signal to one another. Joe had not spent much time with
Matt and Spike through the week, and now they found
themselves walking together. When they stopped for a
picnic lunch, they began talking about their mystery again.
The coded message had been pushed to the back of their
minds with so much else to do at camp.

Now Joe produced his notebook from his backpack and
they pored once again over the clue.

'"Visit the throne on which no king has sat,"'
quoted Joe.

'My gran always calls the loo a throne!' commented
Spike. 'Do you think it means we should look in
the bathroom?'

'I don't think so, unless we have to find a church
dedicated to St Stephen that has a loo!' said Joe.

'I wonder ...' said Matt thoughtfully.

'What do you wonder?' said Joe, turning to his brother.

'Well, do you remember, Spike, the other night when
Tim and Tom were talking about their uncle who was going
to be enthroned as a bishop? I distinctly remember the

word "enthroned". Doesn't that mean he sits on a throne?'

'Wow! You could be right!' exclaimed Spike. 'A bishop sits on a throne on which a king has never sat!'

'I think we have the answer!' said Matt excitedly. 'We have to look for a St Stephen's Cathedral and a bishop's throne!'

'We still have the worst clue of all to decipher,' Joe reminded them. '"Ingaho"!' Whatever does that mean?'

'Ingaho?' said a voice from behind them. 'That's a bit premature! You don't have to say goodbye until tomorrow!'

The three boys looked round, a bit startled. Roy stood behind them.

'How do you know a Kinyarwanda word anyway?' Roy asked them.

He came over and sat with the three boys. They looked at him with mouths open in disbelief. Were they being given their answer just like that?

Matt chuckled. 'We did ask God to tell us what it all meant!' he said.

'What are you on about?' asked Roy, still mystified.

'Can we tell him?' asked Joe.

'I think we'd better,' said Spike, 'since God seems to have sent him with the answer!'

'It's a bit of a long story,' began Joe, 'but we three are a gang called the Whistlers and we have a gang den. One day we found a message in code—we can't really tell you all about that now—but we do know that it was sent by a botanist who was in the Congo somewhere north of a town called Goma. He also sent some letters to Kigali, in Rwanda, to be posted to his nephew. It has taken us most of the summer holiday to break the code and then understand the message.'

Joe got out his notebook again and read the clues
to Roy.

'"Seek and you shall find." We know Jesus said these
words, so we thought that, as well as having to look and
find the answer, the message had something to do with
Christianity in some way.

'"? Perhaps on Boxing Day." This took us longer, but we
decided it was something to do with St Stephen, as Boxing
Day is his feast day. So we thought we had to find a church
dedicated to St Stephen.

'"Visit the throne on which no king has sat." That
clue gave us a lot more problems, but we've just worked
it out—or at least, Matt has. He deduced that we have to
look for a cathedral dedicated to St Stephen and find the
bishop's throne.

'Then the last clue is "ingaho", and we had absolutely
no idea what it could mean until you came up behind us
and asked us why we were saying goodbye!'

Roy was obviously intrigued by the cryptic message.

'Well,' he said, 'if this man was in Congo and sent this
code to Rwanda, I wonder if you'll have to find a cathedral
in Congo or Rwanda.

'I've spent some time in Rwanda during the past two
years—that's how I knew the word was Kinyarwanda for
"goodbye". If he wanted his nephew to look for a cathedral
in Goma, I think he would have used the Swahili word *Kwa
heri* to say goodbye.

'I think it must be a cathedral in Kigali, the capital
of Rwanda.'

Roy sat and thought for a few minutes.

'The cathedral in Kigali, though, is St Michael's. It's Roman Catholic and was built by the Belgians. That doesn't quite fit.

'If you like, when we get home tomorrow, I'll email my friends in Kigali and ask them if they know a St Stephen's Cathedral.'

'Would you really?' said Joe. 'That would be so helpful! But will you keep our secret? We don't want everyone to start looking under the bishop's thrones! We need to be sure before we tell anyone about it.'

'Of course, don't worry,' replied Roy. 'I'll tell you as soon as I have an answer. I expect to be in church every Sunday. Who knows, we could get an answer back very quickly!'

'Time to move !' James's voice called out. 'We want to be back in good time for supper. The cooks are preparing something special for our last night!'

Joe looked at Roy and plucked up courage: 'Roy, could I please walk back with you? I'm not sure about some of the things we've talked about in devotions.'

'Of course!' Roy answered.

Joe looked at Matt and Spike. 'Do you mind if we don't whistle on the way back? I want to spend some time with Roy.'

They began their walk back to camp.

'What's on your mind, Joe?' asked Roy, coming directly to the point. Over the week he had realized that Joe was a bit shy, but also a very thoughtful young man.

'I started coming to church after the Easter holidays,' Joe told him. 'At first I went just because I'd made a promise to Spike when he was in trouble at school. I had to

keep my word, but, to my surprise, I found that church was
not boring! I really liked coming. Then Mum became very
sick. She had a big operation for cancer and then chemo
and radiotherapy. The consultants can't be sure she can be
cured. I found myself praying, and deep down inside I've
felt sure that God has not only heard me, but that, in the
end, Mum will get well. Even when things haven't looked
good, I can't shake off that deep sense of being sure that in
the end she will be OK.

'We prayed together as well, all three of us Whistlers,
that God would help us decipher those clues, and really,
your coming with that last answer has hit me between the
eyes! God must be real to give us an answer like that, and
even though it is just a mystery we are trying to unravel,
he must be interested in us, or he wouldn't bother.

'What is being a Christian really all about? And, if I
become one, how do I do it, and how can I keep it up?'

Roy listened carefully to all Joe had to say. Then he
quietly and simply told Joe again what Jesus's death was
all about. It was as if a light switched on in Joe's mind
and the things he had learned over the past months and
especially through the last week suddenly all made sense.

The rest of the campers were walking ahead of them,
but Roy suggested that he and Joe stop for a few moments.
He gave time to Joe to be quiet and make his own response.
Joe sat and cried as he thought of Jesus being so cruelly
killed on his behalf. He was glad that no one else was there
to see his tears as he prayed for forgiveness for all his
wrong-doing. He asked Jesus to be his Saviour and friend.

Joe just knew that something inside him had changed.
He didn't feel different, but he knew that God had

answered. It was just like when he had prayed for his mum and he knew that all would be well. Joe turned to Roy to say "thank you", only to find that he, too, was wiping tears from his eyes!

'Come on,' said Roy, 'I'll race you to catch up with the others!'

The two of them raced along the cliff path, suddenly full of laughter and happiness. Joe knew without any doubt that he was now a Christian.

When they all arrived back at the campsite they were allowed one last swim.

The cooks had been preparing a fantastic barbeque for supper. Everyone was so happy because it was a fine evening and they could eat outdoors and then have a camp-fire.

After the singing, instead of giving a talk, James and Sue asked if anyone wanted to say a few words about what had been special for them at camp.

Different people had different things to share, some funny and some serious. Joe felt as if his barbeque was churning around inside him. He knew that it was important for him to confess that he had become a Christian. Spike told everyone about his decision after the bullying at school and how camp had helped him to learn more. Eventually, Joe somehow found his voice. It sounded strange, not like his voice at all!

'I came here with lots of questions about Christianity,' he said. 'But Roy has helped me to understand how to become a Christian, and I gave my life over to Jesus when we were out hiking today.'

After a moment's silence that to Joe seemed to last for

ever, Spike began to clap, and everyone else joined in.

It was hard to leave camp, even though Matt and Joe were longing to see their mum again and find out how her latest treatment had gone. Spike was dying to see Tubby and tell him all about the fun they had had at camp. He had really missed his new friend. He laughed inside himself. Who would think he had a friend who was ninety-eight?

Chapter seventeen

T he rest of the summer holidays seemed to fly by! The gang popped in to see Tubby whenever they could, but Spike and Spot were his most regular visitors.

It was a couple of days before school was due to restart when Roy brought some news. After the Sunday service at church, he came into the hall to find the three boys.

'I've got some news for you,' he said. He looked almost as excited as they did. 'My friends in Kigali answered me. They told me that the Episcopal church in Kigali—that's like the Church of England—have a cathedral called St Etienne. At first I was disappointed, because I don't know French, but I've since found out that St Etienne is French for St Stephen!'

'Oh, thanks so much!' said the boys in unison.

'Now we have our answer to the puzzle!' said Joe. 'Of course, being English, Samuel probably went to the Church of England. That is, if he went to a church!'

'What are you going to do with the message?' said Roy. 'If you want my friends to help and try to look for the hidden Christmas present, I promise you that they will be discreet and can be trusted. Of course, after so many years, it may not be there anyway. It's amazing that the cathedral is still standing after the horrors of the genocide in 1994.'

'Thanks for the offer, Roy,' said Joe, looking at the other two Whistlers. 'I think we need a gang meeting to decide what we do next. When we decide, we'll tell you.'

'Fair enough,' answered Roy. 'I shall be interested to know what you say.' Then he waved to the boys as he left the room. 'Ingaho!' he added with a smile.

'Ingaho!' Joe, Matt and Spike replied. Some of the others in the youth group looked at them and asked, 'Whatever was that about?'

'Just saying goodbye in Kinyarwanda,' replied Spike, laughing at their amazed faces.

As the boys started to walk home together, they talked about the coded message.

'We've only got tomorrow and then school starts again,' said Matt. 'I think we should go to the den and discuss what we should do. It seems the appropriate place to make our decision,' he added. 'Maybe we need to do as Tubby suggested: go to visit him first and then go to the den.'

The next day the boys decided to make some sandwiches for a packed lunch, possibly to eat in the park after their meeting. Spike said that he would take Spot with them, knowing that he could leave him with Tubby while they had their gang meeting.

As always, Tubby was pleased to see them.

'Come along in, lads!' he said. They went into the sitting-room, Spike with Spot on his lead.

'Can I leave Spot with you, please, Tubby?' Spike asked. 'We want to go next door for a gang meeting.'

Mr Tibbs's smile suddenly faded. There was no doubt

that he was not happy about the boys going back to the deserted house.

'You have to go there, do you?' he asked. 'I thought perhaps you had forgotten about that place. I tell you, be careful, it's a bad place.'

'We promise we'll be careful. We just need to have our meeting about something. It may even be our last meeting there. You'll have Spot with you. He'll keep you company.'

Joe could see that the old man was still worried.

'What is it, Tubby?' he asked. 'What's worrying you?'

'Nothing really, I'm a silly old man!'

Joe hesitated for a few minutes and then took out his mobile phone.

'I tell you what, Tubby, I'll put my mother's number in the phone here, and if you get worried, all you have to do is press the green little phone picture, you see here?' Joe showed it to Mr Tibbs. 'My mum will be in all day.'

So the boys vaulted the fence in Tubby's garden into the back garden of the deserted house. Had they gone the usual way, they might have seen a black car at the end of The Drive. As it happened, none of them did.

The boys whistled one another in, practising their 'all clear' whistle. They went quietly into the cupboard. On the shelf were their biscuit tin and three cans of lemonade. They took a can each and moved into the kitchen.

'The main purpose of our meeting is to decide what we do with the information we now have,' said Joe. 'We all need to agree on this: Do we let Roy's friends know what we have found out and tell them to look for the Christmas gift mentioned in that coded message, or do we just forget it all, now that we know the truth about this place?'

Matt instantly had his answer: 'I vote we tell them about the message and get them to look.'

Joe looked at them both. 'Let's look at the facts,' he said. 'One. There is no way that we can go and look for ourselves. Two. There may be nothing to find after all these years. Three. If we leave it now, we'll always wonder about it. Four. We did ask God to help us, and it was like a miracle that Roy came along, knew the meaning of the last line of the clue and has friends he can trust who can help us.

'Based on these facts, I think we should trust them to go and look, and then we'll worry about what they find if they find anything.'

'All right, I agree,' said Spike. So they all agreed the way forward. Joe said he would talk to Roy the next Sunday and tell him the full story—or at least, all that they knew about the house and its occupants—and get him to ask his friends to make a search.

Joe put his notebook away and they were just opening their cans when they heard a noise. They froze! Someone was opening the front door. It was so unexpected that they didn't have the presence of mind to try to get back into the cupboard and out through the window.

'The Matshimbi diamond must be here in this house,' said a deep voice in a strange accent.

'We'll turn the place upside down until we find it!' another voice said. The boys didn't dare make a sound. They looked at one another fearfully.

Matt was the first to move. With a finger to his lips, he began to walk towards the door to go to the cupboard, and the others began to follow. As they did so, the kitchen door opened and two men appeared!

The men were as startled by the boys as the boys had been by them. Matt made a run for the door, but he was quickly grabbed by the largest of the men, who was black-skinned and spoke with a heavy accent.

'Not so fast, young man. You're going nowhere!'

As Spike then tried to rush out, the other, smaller man pulled a gun from his pocket.

'None of you move!' he shouted. 'What are you doing here?' he demanded.

Joe tried to stay calm, but his heart was racing wildly and his mouth was dry.

'We use this room for our gang den,' he said truthfully. 'We're not up to any harm.'

'We'll see about that!' said the first man roughly. 'What do you know about this place?' He shook Matt's arm, demanding an answer.

'Well, it's just a deserted house!' Matt answered. 'Please let go of my arm, you're hurting me!'

'What shall we do with them?' the dark man asked the smaller one with the gun.

'We'll take them hostage,' he answered. 'Take them into the dining-room and tie them up while we turn the place over. I guess they know something or they wouldn't be here!'

The smaller man, who to Joe looked like a gypsy by his size and colouring, pushed him forward and then indicated to Spike and Matt to follow Joe into the dining-room. The small man knew his way around the house, Joe noted.

The boys were lined up against the wall. All three were very scared. The black man, who Matt thought must be

an African, went out, presumably to his car, and came
back with thick ropes. He then tied the boys to chairs.
When they were all securely fastened, the African began to
interrogate them.

Who were they? Why did they come to this house? How
did they get in? What had they found there? Where was the
treasure hidden?

The boys kept silent. This made him very angry and he
started hitting them.

Suddenly Spike whistled. It was the bird-call that they
used to say 'keep quiet'.

'Shut up! Are you cheeking me?' the African said as
he heard the whistle, and he whacked Spike's face so that
blood trickled down from his mouth. 'You cheek me and
nobody will recognize your face!' he threatened.

'Come on, they're only local brats. Let's search this
place and worry about them after. That diamond must be
hidden here somewhere.'

'And you shut up too,' the African bellowed at the other
man. 'We don't want them knowing what we're up to!'

They turned from the boys and started to empty every
drawer and cupboard. The dust swirled around. It made
them all splutter and sneeze, but poor Joe began to wheeze.
Matt looked at him in fear. He knew how quickly Joe could
develop a severe asthma attack.

'Please, please let my brother go. He's having an asthma
attack!' pleaded Matt to the two men.

'So, you've got a voice, then?' the black man snarled at
him. 'Tell us what we want to know and we might think
about it!' He laughed a horrible laugh.

Joe was getting worse and worse. His lips were going

blue and his breaths were coming in shallow gasps. The man with the gun looked at him and then asked him if he had some medicine.

Joe was almost unconscious, and certainly unable to talk, but Matt pointed to his pocket where Joe kept his inhaler. The man reached for it and tried to make Joe inhale it as best he could. The African man got impatient and told him to leave him and search another room. Both men then left the room.

The boys were so glad to be left on their own. Matt was frightened about Joe's condition, but he was trying not to panic.

'We have a weapon we haven't used,' whispered Spike. 'We can pray.' Both boys began to mutter prayers as they cried out for help in their situation. Then Spike took the initiative again.

'Remember the story of Paul when he was imprisoned?' he said. 'He sang! Let's sing, just like we did at camp.'

Matt thought Spike was going crazy, but anything was worth trying. Spike struck up with a song they had learnt round the camp-fire.

'Praise the name of Jesus,
Praise the name of Jesus,
He's my rock, he's my fortress,
He's my deliverer,
In him will I trust.
Praise the name of Jesus!'

They kept singing it over and over like a prayer. The more they sang, the less Matt found his legs were shaking.

The panic inside him subsided a little. They could hear
banging and swearing coming from upstairs. It sounded as
if the floorboards were being ripped out!

Chapter eighteen

Spike and Matt lost sense of time. It seemed as if they had been tied up for hours. Joe was unconscious but still breathing. In spite of the noise upstairs, Spike heard a wonderful sound: he heard Spot's bark! It was followed by the sirens of police cars. Someone approached the front door, but the African and gypsy greeted whoever it was with a gun. The policeman was pushed into the dining-room and was about to be tied up with the boys.

Spike was softly whistling in the way he whistled to Spot, for he knew that Spot was around somewhere. The African had the rope and was about to tie up the policeman, so the gunman hit Spike again on the face to make him stop. When he struck Spike, something flew at his feet and he yelped out in pain, dropping the gun. In a flash, the policeman grabbed the gun and turned it on the men. Spot was growling and baring his teeth at them.

In seconds the house was swarming with policemen. The boys were quickly untied and a paramedic was soon helping Joe. He was taken to an ambulance. Joe and Matt's mum and dad were standing by, looking very anxious. Matt ran to his mum and was so glad to receive her hug! Spike's family were there too, and Mr Tibbs. Once the boys had been comforted by their parents, a policeman told Matt and Spike that they had to go to the hospital to be checked. Afterwards, there would be plenty of time to talk, and the police would want to hear their story.

Joe went to the hospital in the ambulance with his dad, while the other boys went in a car with their parents. The two prisoners were taken in a police van to the police station, and dear old Tubby took care of Spot, who was really the hero of the day!

Matt was fine. Spike had bruises on his face and his mouth was swollen, but there was no serious damage. Joe was slowly improving, but was kept in hospital.

'No school for you tomorrow!' commented his dad, as Joe was settled into a bed.

'I'm not sure about you two going either,' said the policeman. 'We need to talk to the three of you and get statements. I need to know what you were up to in that house, anyway!'

Matt and Spike looked at each other. They knew they had been trespassing, and they could be in serious trouble! The policeman gave them a wink and a smile, which made them feel a little better. Then Matt and Spike were allowed home.

'I guess we'd better hear the whole story,' said Spike's dad. 'I know Joe's not here, but at least you two can put us in the picture. Thank goodness Joe had left his mobile with Mr Tibbs!'

After they had gone into the deserted house, Mr Tibbs had a feeling that all was not well. Even Spot was restless and kept prowling around, and then he began to growl.

Although Tubby was quite deaf, he heard some banging coming from next door. He went outside to hear a little better, and was really alarmed by the banging, shouting and swearing. He realized that something was happening, so he lifted Spot over the fence and then went to phone Joe's mum, who immediately phoned the police, her husband and the Frasers. Mrs Jones had little to go on, but she told the officer that she understood the boys were in some sort of serious trouble in the deserted house at the end of The Drive. She also told the police that Joe suffered from severe asthma, and that any stress might provoke an attack, so they called for an ambulance to attend the scene.

Nobody seemed too angry with Matt and Spike, much to their relief. Their parents were just glad that their sons were safe. The boys began to tell their story, but it came out in bits and pieces, and the shock of what had happened had left them a bit confused. In the end, Mr Fraser suggested that they wait until the next day when hopefully Joe would also be home and they could tell their story more coherently.

Matt and Spike were fine the next morning. They ran down the road to see Tubby.

'The police have cordoned off the house,' Mr Tibbs said. 'The press have been here taking photographs, and even the TV people are here. I hope they pull it down now!'

The boys had to sneak out of Tubby's house, glad of their 'all clear' whistles to help each other get into The Drive without any reporters seeing who they were.

After lunch, Joe came home and then the police arrived to take their statements.

The boys told the story, right from the very first ball

being kicked into the garden. Joe's notebook was very useful and the policeman commended him for his good deductions. Joe handed over the two letters which he had taken from the cardboard box in the guest-room, together with their interpretation of the coded message. They told the policeman about Roy and the deduction that the 'Christmas gift' was in Rwanda.

The policeman told them that they had questioned the two men who had been caught at the house, and they admitted to trying to steal a huge diamond that had been taken from Matshimbi, in Congo, many years previously. The men thought it must be hidden in the house. One of them men was Congolese and had tried to search the house some years previously. At that time he had little English, so had ignored the letters in the box. He admitted to leaving some witch-doctor's curses in the dining-room, which he believed would protect him when he returned and curse anyone else who entered the house. He had returned to the Congo, but after a long time he was contacted by the gypsy, who was a relative of Lucy's. Together they were determined at all costs to find the Matshimbi diamond for themselves!

The policeman told the boys quite gently that they had, of course, been trespassing, but all things considered, no charges would be brought against them. They might be required at a later date to give evidence in court, but they must be very careful not to tell the full story to the press. They were merely to say that they had used the old house as a den.

Things calmed down after a few days, as they always do, and the press stopped bothering the boys. At first it was

embarrassing at school, at church, and even walking up
The Drive. They were glad when life went back to normal.

Detectives had been sent to Rwanda, and they eventually
found, ingeniously set into the wood on the underside of
the bishop's throne in St Stephen's Cathedral, the huge
Matshimbi diamond. It was returned to the Congolese
government, to whom it rightfully belonged. There was a
substantial reward for its recovery, and this was given to
the Whistlers!

One of the detectives visited the boys to give them
the reward. He was able to tell them a little more of the
story. Apparently, Stephen Jenkins had been approached
by a very wealthy American who coveted the Matshimbi
diamond, offering him a huge amount of money if he would
steal it. Stephen so wanted to restore his family fortunes
that he undertook the mission, even though he knew it was
wrong to do so. He then hid the diamond in the cathedral
because he realized that some Congolese people suspected
him of the crime. Even though some years had elapsed,
they never gave up the quest to retrieve the diamond,
sending one of the young men of their village to England
to search for it. On his first visit he had learnt about the
family history and contacted the gypsies. One of Lucy's
relatives was only too eager to help him, hoping for a huge
reward. He and his friend were the two men who were
arrested by the police at the deserted house.

The detectives had other news that really pleased the
Whistlers: in their investigations they had managed to find
Lucy and Paul. They were living quietly and very happily
in a cottage in the country, and they had two sons who
were about the ages of Spike and Matt. They were glad to

hear that the diamond had been found and returned to its rightful owners. They asked that the old house be sold and the money given to charity; they wanted nothing more to do with it.

They gang met to decide how to use their reward money. They asked Roy to help them choose a project in Africa to which they could donate it. They decided to help orphans in Rwanda.

After the trial, both men were sentenced to long terms of imprisonment. Roy, because of his African connections, had begun to take an interest in the Congolese prisoner and he regularly visited him. He was still mystified as to why the powerful curses which he had left in the dining-room had not worked. One day, Roy asked the boys again what exactly had happened when they were taken hostage in that room. Spike told them how he and Matt had prayed, and they had then sung the song they had learnt around the camp-fire about the name of Jesus.

A huge smile broke over Roy's face.

'That's the answer!' he said. 'The name of Jesus is more powerful than any other power in heaven or on earth!'

'I really thought Joe was going to die,' admitted Matt, 'and I thought we might be shot as well. I vowed to God that, if he would get us out of that mess, then I would follow him too, like Spike and Joe. I'm a Christian now too!'

Spike beamed at his best friend. Everything had been worthwhile!

After the trial the deserted house was demolished. The happiest person of all was Mr Tibbs! He had hated that house ever since the first death there. Builders arrived and put up a block of apartments in its place, but they left the beautiful Wattle tree. Each time the boys went past the new development, the tree reminded them of their adventure and the mystery of the deserted house!

About Day One:

Day One's threefold commitment:

~ To be faithful to the Bible, God's inerrant, infallible Word;

~ To be relevant to our modern generation;

~ To be excellent in our publication standards.

I continue to be thankful for the publications of Day One. They are biblical; they have sound theology; and they are relative to the issues at hand. The material is condensed and manageable while, at the same time, being complete—a challenging balance to find. We are happy in our ministry to make use of these excellent publications.

JOHN MACARTHUR, PASTOR-TEACHER,
GRACE COMMUNITY CHURCH, CALIFORNIA

It is a great encouragement to see Day One making such excellent progress. Their publications are always biblical, accessible and attractively produced, with no compromise on quality. Long may their progress continue and increase!

JOHN BLANCHARD, AUTHOR, EVANGELIST AND APOLOGIST

Visit our website for more information and to request a free catalogue of our books.

www.dayone.co.uk